BAR AUNT BOOMERANG

When a giant shoe shop sign fell from its hinges during the filming of the 3013th episode of the Aussi soap, Cobblers, it dropped straight onto actress Celia Bigsby's head.

It proved a fatal blow.

Furious that her death had robbed her of her adoring fans, Celia Bigsby decided to return to life as the ghost of her soap opera character, Aunt Boomerang. Her mission: to use her ghostly powers to turn scaredy-cats into daredevils.

First published in Great Britain in 1999
The Limerick Book Publishing Company, 58 Llanvanor Road, London NW2 2AP

The moral right of the author has been asserted
A CIP catalogue record of this book is available from the British Library

ISBN 1 190 879 36 4

Designed by Judith Stevens

Printed in Great Britain by
T.J. International, Cornwall

To Barry Cunningham

... the third man

From the BBC TV Series

BARMY AUNT BOOMERANG

... The Soap Star Ghost ...

by

ROY APPS

drawings by

Dorian Aroyo

C O N T

E N T S

In the sun's solar system is a small planet known as Earth.

In the top half of Earth is a continent known as Europe.

In the top corner of Europe is a country known as Scotland.

In Scotland is a city known as Glasgow.

In Glasgow is a street known as Tannochbrae Close.

In Tannochbrae Close is a house known as Number 40.

In Number 40 live the Simpkins family: dad Kevin, mum Tracey and their son Sebastian.

With the Simpkins family lives the ghost of an Australian soap star known to everyone as barmy Aunt Boomerang.

Chapter 1

THE MAN IN BLACK

1

The Man in Black

Aunt Boomerang stood at her bedroom window and breathed in the crisp morning air. She looked out at the orangey-red bricked houses in Tannochbrae Close. In the three weeks or so since she had arrived, completely unannounced, she had grown rather fond of the odd little semi-detached house with its pointy gables and wonky chimney. She had also grown fond of its inhabitants, Kev and Tracey Simpkins, and their eleven year old son Sebastian.

In fact, *so* fond had she become of them, that she had given them all presents. For dad Kev, a workbench and tool kit; for mum Tracey, a potter's wheel and kiln. As for Sebastian, she had given him *two* presents.

One was a bamboo whistle decorated with green leaves.

"It's an ancient instrument," Aunt Boomerang had explained, "that I learnt how to make from the native Australians. You could blow one of these at Gobbagobba Hill and it would be heard five hundred miles away at Kookaburra Creek. If you ever need the help of an old Australian Aunt, just give a small blast."

The other present had been equally special. Using the

ancient powers she had learnt while staying with native Australians in the outback, Aunt Boomerang had turned Sebastian from a scaredy-cat into a daredevil. Well, almost.

"I think I'll drift up to the school to watch Sebastian at football practice this afternoon," she said to herself. "But for the rest of the day I'm just going to float about taking things nice and easy."

Which goes to show just how wrong you can be. Even when you're the ghost of an Australian soap star.

"Sebby, it's your ball!"

Sebastian Simpkins, fair-haired and freckled, raced towards the football bobbing up and down a couple of metres in front of him. It was Meryl's Marvels' final practice before the Five-a-Side Football Competition.

Now, you may think that "Meryl's Marvels" is a bit of a daft name for a football team. It doesn't, after all, have the exciting ring of "Manchester United" about it. Still less, the thrilling brevity of "Celtic". But Meryl's Marvels were called "Meryl's Marvels" for two very good reasons:

One – They were marvels. At least, they thought they were. They had already beaten three other teams to reach the five-a-side final.

Two – They were captained by Sebastian's friend, Meryl Mackintosh. Meryl was in Sebastian's class. She had straight dark hair and large brown, sad-looking eyes. Sebastian and his classmates called her Merry. This was because her name was Meryl. For, although her nickname was Merry, it was most definately not her nature. Meryl tended to sigh a lot: she was someone who was always expecting the worst.

"Sebby!" she yelled.

Sebastian swung back his right leg and gave the ball an almighty thump. It curled agonisingly slowly through the air. Then, as it reached the top of its arc, it hung there for a moment before dropping over the keeper's head and into the goal. It would have hit the net, but they didn't have nets on the goalposts at Millstone School. It was a goal, nevertheless.

"Y-E-E-E-H!" yelled Sebastian, jigging about in celebratory dance.

"Oh dear," groaned Meryl with her customary gloomy sigh.

"Merry, I scored!" trumpeted Sebastian, his face flushed pink with excitement.

"I know you did, Sebby."

"Then why aren't you cheering me?"

"Because you scored at the wrong end!"

"Ah ... "

Before Sebastian could say anymore, their class teacher, Ms Goodbody, was blowing on her whistle.

"OK, Meryl's Marvels. That's it for today. All the best for the final tomorrow."

Mr Norman Diplock MA, Head Teacher at Millstone School, was known by teachers and children alike as Old Dipstick. He had the kind of face which made him look like a cross between Darth Maul and Quasi Modo.

Old Dipstick's office window overlooked the school playing field. Standing with him at his office window was Councillor Mrs Margaret Belcher, Chair of the School Governors. She had the kind of face which made her look like a cross between Darth Maul and Darth Maul's mum. In fact, she *wasn't* Darth Maul's mum. She was Ashley Belcher's mum.

"If that's the team my little Ashley and his friends are up against tomorrow, his team won't have any trouble winning," Mrs Belcher sneered. She paused and shot Old Dipstick a threatening look. "Anyway, I'm sure the man in black will see to it that the right team wins."

"The man in black?" Old Dipstick's knowledge of football slang was sketchy, to say the least.

"The referee!"

"Ah yes, of course." Old Dipstick furrowed his brow. "But *I* am the referee!"

"Precisely," snapped Mrs Belcher. "And it's your job to make sure that my little Ashley gets a winning captain's medal!"

Outside on the football pitch, Mrs Belcher's little Ashley, captain of Belcher's Belters, grinned the kind of evil little grin you can only manage if you're a genuine numero uno ugly brute and premier school bully. His eyes were on the far side of the pitch where Sebastian was busy practising his ball skills. The other Marvels, Jas, Pandora and Jodie, turned from watching him. They gathered round their captain.

"He's got to go, Merry," said Jodie. A tall, older-looking girl, she was a star of the school drama club. She mimicked Sebastian's movements as they watched him fall over the ball - yet again.

"Don't know why you picked him," muttered Jas, a keen footballer who kept an autographed photo of Dwight Yorke in his schoolbag.

"She fancies him," replied Jodie.

"I don't," retorted Meryl with a blush.

"They're right, Merry," said Pandora, the goalkeeper, pouting. She pulled off her gloves and threw them on the ground. "If Sebastian's in our team tomorrow, there's no point any of us turning up."

"We've got this far with him," pointed out Meryl, anxious to protect her friend.

"Aye, but we'll not beat Belcher's Belters," reasoned Jas.

"Who would *you* pick in Sebastian's place, then?" asked Meryl, a trifle huffily.

All eyes turned to the far end of the field. A small lad, barely the height of a corner flag, juggled a ball expertly between his feet.

"Wee Hamish!" said Jas, Jodie and Pandora in unison.

"He is good," admitted Meryl with a sad sigh.

"Right," said Jodie, quickly. "Go and tell Sebastian he's dropped."

"Me?" gasped Meryl in alarm.

"Of course, *you*," shrugged Jodie unsympathetically. "*You're* the captain."

Jodie, Jas and Pandora wandered off. Meryl flopped down on the pitch, exhausted not just by football practice, but by the thought of having to tell her best friend that, when it came to football, he was a dumbo.

"Oh dear," she said to herself. "I can't tell him." Then she noticed Sebastian's jacket lying screwed up on the ground where he'd left it. Sticking out of the pocket was a bamboo whistle, Sebastian's billabong blaster. Meryl's frown faded. "But I know someone who can!"

Meryl knew all about Sebastian's billabong blaster. She had been there when Sebastian had used it to call up Aunt Boomerang. Deftly, she slipped the billabong blaster from Sebastian's pocket into her own.

Sebastian sauntered over and picked up his jacket. He turned to Meryl.

"You coming?"

Meryl shook her head, too full of anguish to look him in the eye.

"Got to work out tactics for tomorrow, eh?"

Meryl nodded. "Aye," she said without looking up. "Something like that."

She waited until Sebastian was out of sight. Then she took the billabong blaster, put it to her lips and blew hard. There was a misty shimmering in front of her. Out of the shimmering appeared the smiling, comforting figure of Aunt Boomerang, her red velvet gown billowing in the breeze.

"High Noon, sweetheart?" she asked. High Noon was any time you had something really hard to do or to decide about. High Noon was the time when you needed Aunt Boomerang.

"High Noon, Aunt Boomerang," nodded Meryl sadly.

Aunt Boomerang grinned, then winked encouragingly at Meryl. "Best sit down next to me and tell me about it then," she said.

Something was cooking in the Simpkins' kitchen.

"Smells good, Mum. What is it?" asked Sebastian, trying to make himself heard above the noise of his rumbling stomach.

"Aunt Boomerang's given your dad a tool kit and work bench and me a potter's wheel and kiln." Mrs Simpkins pulled open the door of her potter's kiln. "And what's cooking is ... two mugs, three cups and thirteen garden gnomes," she declared proudly, sliding out a tray of baked pottery.

Sebastian looked at the gnomes. Their faces resembled the gargoyles that medieval stonemasons carved to scare the devil away.

"They've got the faces of different TV personalities on them," Mrs Simpkins explained. Mrs Simpkins was very keen on TV personalities. "This one's Cilla Black."

"Cilla Black? Looks more like Godzilla Black," replied Sebastian, making a swift exit before his mum had time to catch exactly what he had said.

In the lounge, Sebastian found his dad mending the sideboard. Now, although he knew little about DIY, Sebastian had seen enough episodes of *Changing Rooms* to know that mending sideboards required equipment like clamps and wood glue. Mr Simpkins was using a hammer and a pack of ten centimetre long nails.

"Yee-oww! Blast!" yelled Mr Simpkins as, for a change, he stopped hitting a ten centimetre long nail and started hitting a five centimetre long thumb.

Mr Simpkins was no better at DIY than Mrs Simpkins was at pottery.

"Amazing," thought Sebastian, "how people can think they're good at something, when actually they're really naff." Obviously, something had to be done. At this rate, it was only a matter of time before his dad ruined every piece of furniture in the house and his mum filled the kitchen with Carol Vorderman gravy boats. Sebastian put his hand in his jacket pocket. It was empty.

"My billabong blaster! It must've fallen out of my pocket on the playing field!"

And with that, he rushed out of the house and headed for the school playing fields.

" ... The trouble is, Aunt Boomerang," sighed Meryl, "I can't tell Sebby he's completely useless at football. It would hurt him so much." She paused. "But you can."

"Can I, sweetheart?" asked Aunt Boomerang with a frown.

"Of course you can! You're a ghost; you don't have feelings."

"Merry, sweetheart, ghost I may be, but I can't tell Sebastian he's dropped from the football team."

"But why not?"

"Because *you're* the captain."

"That's what the others said," muttered Merry.

"And," continued Aunt Boomerang, "you're his friend. His *best* friend. You're the *only* person who can tell him."

Meryl looked up and saw Sebastian approaching, head down, scouring the ground for his lost billabong blaster.

"It's here, sweetheart!" Aunt Boomerang called, waving the billabong blaster. "You must've dropped it. You really must look after it."

Meryl looked sheepish as Aunt Boomerang caught her

eye.

"Got to shoot," she said, giving Meryl a big, encouraging wink. And with that she - quite literally - disappeared.

"Got the tactics sorted?" asked Sebastian, sitting down next to Meryl.

Meryl nodded slowly. Seriously. "Aye. Got the tactics sorted."

"Great team we've got, isn't it?" Sebastian continued.

"No," said Meryl flatly. "It isn't."

"Pandora in goal, Jas as sweeper, me up front -" He paused. "Pardon?"

"No Sebby. It's not a great team we've got. It's a lousy team. Someone's got to go."

Sebastian frowned at Meryl, "Not Jas?"

"Not Jas."

"Pandora?"

"No."

"Surely not Jodie?"

"No!"

Sebastian stared at Meryl wide-eyed. "Merry, you can't ... no, surely you're not dropping ... *yourself?*"

Meryl looked steadily and sadly at Sebastian. "No Sebby. I'm dropping *you.*"

Sebastian stood with his mouth wide open. He looked like a goldfish - a gormless goldfish. He tried to speak, but found the words wouldn't come.

"Sebby, you're good at lots of things ... acting ... telling jokes ... mountain biking ... being a daredevil ... being a mate ... ". She paused before adding, "But you're rubbish at football."

"All right," muttered Sebastian, pouting his lips, "so I'm a bit rusty."

"A *bit* rusty? Sebby, you're as rusty as the wreck of the Titanic!"

There were tears in Sebastian's eyes. He'd not cried in front of a girl since the Infants. Meryl grabbed his sleeve.

"Sebby, we can still be mates ... "

Sebastian shook her off roughly. "Gerroff you!" he sobbed. And he ran off across the playing field.

Meryl sat alone on the edge of the pitch. She'd hurt her best friend's feelings. He probably wouldn't want to speak to her again - ever. And she couldn't really blame him.

Aunt Boomerang knew that Sebastian was in his room, but she waited until the sun had gone down before she knocked on his door.

"What?" enquired a miserable voice.

Aunt Boomerang walked through the door into Sebastian's room. She often used her ghostly powers to walk through doors. It saved her he trouble of having to open them.

"I don't understand it," Sebastian sighed.

"I think you do, sweetheart."

Sebastian frowned. He took it for granted that Aunt Boomerang knew exactly what he was talking about. Being a ghost with magical powers, she always did.

"Have you seen your mum's pots?" enquired Aunt Boomerang.

"Aye, they look like blobs of that plastic dog poo you get in joke shops," said Sebastian grimly, "but she thinks they're wonderful."

Aunt Boomerang nodded. "Have you seen your dad's DIY?"

"Terrible," sighed Sebastian. "But he thinks he's the new Handy Andy."

"Amazing, isn't it," said Aunt Boomerang, "how people can think they're good at something when actually they're really rubbish."

But Sebastian wasn't listening. "Aunt Boomerang!" he said excitedly. "You have powers!"

Aunt Boomerang nodded.

"You turned Ashley Belcher into a Madagascan cock-roach - "

"For three seconds, yes ... "

"You could turn me into a really brilliant footballer!"

Now it was Aunt Boomerang's turn to sigh. "Sebastian, sweetheart, I have the power to turn Belchers into cockroaches and scaredy-cats into daredevils. But there is no way I could turn you into a decent footballer. Not even for three seconds."

"Are you sure, Aunt Boomerang?" asked Sebastian desperately.

"I'm sure. Believe me." She sighed again. "I've seen you play."

Aunt Boomerang looked at Sebastian's bookshelves. Grouped on the top shelf were a handful of books all concerned with the Rules of the Scottish Football Association.

"Do you know all the rules?"

"Of course I do."

Aunt Boomerang's face broke out into a wry smile. "I have just thought of Plan A. Be at the match tomorrow - "

"No way!" interrupted Sebastian fiercely. "Merry's dropped me from the team, remember? I'll be a laughing stock. I'm staying here!"

"Sweetheart, I can't turn you into a footballer, but you can play in the five-a-side final tomorrow."

"Can I?"

"If you're daredevil enough to brave the taunts and turn up for the match." Aunt Boomerang looked deeply into Sebastian's eyes. "Sebastian ... you are a daredevil ... "

Sebastian held Aunt Boomerang's look. There still seemed to be doubt in his eyes.

Old Dipstick was in his office early the next day. From his kit bag he took out a gold medal the size of a Wagon Wheel. It was inscribed "Presented to the Referee: Millstone School Five-a-Side Football Competition". Old Dipstick kissed the medal, then placed it around his neck. He tucked it out of the way under his shirt. Then he turned and went outside in search of some small Year Three boys to shout at for playing in the playground.

Suddenly, a ghostly figure in a flowing red gown walked through the wall into Old Dipstick's office. She took Old Dipstick's black referee's kit from his bag and disappeared back through the wall.

That lunchtime, Aunt Boomerang pulled Old Dipstick's kit from the washing machine where she had cold rinsed it. She popped it into the pottery kiln, turned the dial to "High" and waited.

A couple of hours later, the kit was back in Old Dipstick's bag.

Merry's Marvels and Belcher's Belters were warming up on the touchline.

"Who was dropped from the team? Who was dropped from the team?" chanted Ashley and his mates as Sebastian made his lonely way past them to the watching crowd. He wished he was anywhere else but here. The thought even crossed his mind that he had been better off as a scaredy-cat. He stared glumly down at his feet. How could Aunt Boomerang possibly get him a game? Meryl was right; he was useless.

A cheer went up as the referee came out. The cheer quickly turned to guffaws of laughter. Old Dipstick's referee's shirt barely covered his chest! Below the black shirt was a gap revealing fifteen centimetres of white thermal vest. He was walking like a constipated robot.

Sebastian looked up and saw Aunt Boomerang standing beside him, a wide grin on her face.

"Honey," she whispered, "I shrunk the kit!"

Ms Goodbody stared at Old Dipstick. "Mr Diplock, you cannot possibly referee a football match like that!"

"I don't understand," whined Old Dipstick. "It was fine when I tried it on this morning!"

"Well, it's not now," snorted Ms Goodbody. She turned to the crowd. "Is there anybody here who knows the rules of five-a-side football and who could step into that kit?" She pointed to the child-sized garments Old Dipstick was wearing.

Sebastian felt an enormous shove between his shoulder blades.

"Told you I'd get you a game!" Aunt Boomerang whispered in his ear.

Sebastian enjoyed being a referee. He did well. He kept the game flowing. He was quick to spot offsides. He was even quicker to send Ashley off for his second blatant foul on Wee Hamish.

For the record, Merry's Marvels beat Belcher's Belters 14-6. With undisguised ill-grace, Old Dipstick presented Merry's Marvels with their medals. He turned quickly to go, only to find Ms Goodbody blocking his path.

"Isn't there a ref's medal?" she asked him pointedly.

Old Dipstick clenched his fists. Then, cursing under his breath, he put his hand down the front of his shirt and hauled out his prized gold medal as big as a Wagon Wheel.

"Hadn't you better put it round the ref's neck?" suggested Ms Goodbody.

"I'd rather shove it down his throat," muttered Old Dipstick as he placed it around Sebastian's neck.

Staggering under the weight of their medals, Sebastian and Meryl strolled home with Aunt Boomerang.

"Sebby, you may be a lousy footballer, but you're an ace ref," said Meryl admiringly.

Sebastian shrugged. "Thanks to Aunt Boomerang," he said.

"You made it possible, Sebastian, you daredevil," said Aunt Boomerang. "It took some guts to go along to that match, knowing you would be laughed at for being dropped from the team. Talking of guts, did you see Old Dipstick's vest?"

Meryl and Sebastian nodded, before bursting out into uncontrollable laughter at the very thought of it.

Old Dipstick turned the handle of his office door. At last, the nightmare was over and he could be alone. He stepped into his office - and saw Councillor Mrs Belcher sitting at his desk. He knew straightaway that the nightmare *wasn't* over.

"You promised my little Ashley a medal!" she hissed accusingly.

"I promised *myself* a medal!" replied Old Dipstick. "It was the Pumpkins boy's barmy Aunt Boogiebong. She's trouble. And I don't like trouble! I don't know how she did it, but she shrunk my referee's kit!"

"What are you going to do about it?" asked Mrs Belcher.

"I'm going to get myself another medal," exclaimed Old Dipstick.

"I meant about my little Ashley!" roared Mrs Belcher.

"I'll make him register monitor for the rest of the week," grumbled Old Dipstick.

"Just you make sure you do," threatened Mrs Belcher huffily. "I am a town councillor and *Chair* of the School Governors!" And she turned and marched straight out.

Old Dipstick grunted grumpily to himself. "I *will* get myself a medal," he snarled. "Oh yes!"

Chapter 2

MUD, SWEAT AND GEARS

2

Mud, Sweat and Gears

"I *will* get myself a medal. Oh yes!" Old Dipstick's blazing eyes stared madly across his desk at Councillor Mrs Belcher. "The *Golden Stick of Chalk Award* judges are visiting the school next Monday," he continued.

"*Golden Stick of Chalk Award*?" enquired Mrs Belcher.

"The award for the most efficient school in the land." His eyes stared out like two glassy marbles. "Which *I* am going to win!"

"Correction, Norman," interrupted Mrs Belcher. "Which *we* are going to win. I am Chair of the School Governors."

"Of course, Margaret." Old Dipstick squirmed a little in his chair. "Which *we* are going to win!" There was a distinct twitch in his eye as he added, "And that Pumpkin boy's barmy Aunt Bimboobong won't stop me this time!"

Meryl Mackintosh stopped her bike at the bottom of the hill and looked behind her. Sebastian was nowhere to be seen. She sighed. It had been Sebastian's idea to have a bike race. She would have been happy with a leisurely ride around the park. But, since Aunt Boomerang had turned Sebastian from a weasely scaredy-cat into a dashing daredevil he had become, well ... not to put too fine a point on it, *big headed* was the only word for it.

Meryl waited until Sebastian appeared breathless at the top of the hill behind her, then she pedalled on, round a tight corner and into the small wood on the edge of the park. "Some race," she thought. Suddenly she saw her way blocked by a large fallen branch. She braked just in time to stop herself going head first over her handlebars.

From the other side of the branch appeared three familiar figures.

"If it isn't the famous footballing heroine!" Ashley Belcher grinned his favourite evil little grin. The kind of evil little grin you can only manage if you're, well, Ashley Belcher.

"Out on your lonesome, then?" enquired the genuine numero uno ugly brute and bully.

Sebastian rode up beside Meryl, still breathless despite the fact that the last two hundred metres of his ride had been *down*hill.

"I'll leave you to your boyfriend, then," Ashley muttered to Meryl.

Sebastian suddenly found his voice. "She's not my girlfriend!" he shouted.

Meryl winced. She wasn't Sebastian's girlfriend - at least she didn't think she was, but she wished he hadn't sounded quite so appalled at the thought. She shot Sebastian a frosty look. He didn't see her. He was looking at Ashley's brand new mountain bike.

"Smart, eh," said Ashley. "It'd beat that old heap of yours any day."

"What are you calling an old heap?" retorted Sebastian, suddenly all fired up.

"That!" laughed Ashley, pointing to Sebastian's machine.

In truth, Sebastian's bike with its hub gears, rusting wheels and mudguards tied on with string could have been called a lot worse things than 'an old heap".

"Wanna bet?" challenged Sebastian.

"Sebby!" hissed Meryl in alarm. If Sebastian couldn't even keep up with her in a bike race, what chance had he against Ashley Belcher and his mountain bike?

"Round the park, through the new estate and finishing up at school," said Ashley. "Monday, after school."

"You're on," said Sebastian.

"What'll you bet?"

"Anything!"

Ashley paused, then grinned slyly. "Your magic flute thing?"

"OK!" Sebastian said without flinching.

Meryl gasped. She couldn't believe it. Sebastian had agreed to a stupid bike race with Ashley Belcher which he had no chance of winning. Not only that, he had bet what

Ashley called "the magic flute thing". What Ashley called "the magic flute thing" was, of course, the billabong blaster. Meryl got on her bike and pedalled for all she was worth towards Sebastian's house. There was only one person who could help now.

"Woggling wallabies!" exclaimed Aunt Boomerang when Meryl had told her what Sebastian had done. Her pale eyes widened to such an extent Meryl thought they were going to pop out. "If the billabong blaster falls into Ashley Belcher's hands, it'll mean he could beam me up like a genie any time he wanted!" Her body trembled with a ghostly shiver. "My after-life won't be worth living! Come on, we've got to find Sebby!"

They found Sebastian training. He was riding his bike round and round the school field.

"I've seen slugs move faster," sighed Aunt Boomerang.

"Oh dear," sighed Meryl. "What are we going to do?"

But Aunt Boomerang wasn't listening. She'd noticed a car in the staff car park - Old Dipstick's car.

"Old Dipstick at school? On a Saturday? Something's going on. And if it involves Old Dipstick, the chances are it's more fishy than a plate of rotting kippers. Wait here, sweetheart."

"Aunt Boomerang, what about the bike race and the billabong blaster?" called Meryl desperately.

But Aunt Boomerang had disappeared – literally – into thin air.

Old Dipstick sat in his office and looked across his desk at Councillor Mrs Belcher.

"I've been thinking about this *Golden Stick of Chalk Award*, Norman. We do have a major problem," Mrs Belcher was saying.

"We do ...?"

"We do. The judges will expect the grounds and the buildings to be bursting with bright and fragrant flowers." Mrs Belcher lifted a sad looking plant pot from the window sill. "All you have is one cactus that looks like a dead hedgehog!"

"Plants cost money, Margaret. I don't like spending money." Old Dipstick shivered at the thought.

"Correction, Norman," smiled Mrs Belcher. "You don't like spending *your* money. Supposing the money for the plants and flowers belonged to somebody else..."

Old Dipstick followed her gaze to a brass piggy bank on the side cupboard.

"You don't mean the School Fund?"

Mrs Belcher nodded. "It usually pays for the Christmas Party and other treats for the children, doesn't it?"

It was Old Dipstick's turn to nod. "There's always trouble

at the Christmas Party. And I don't like trouble. In fact, I like it even less than spending money!" He paused. "You think I should take the School Fund to buy plants and flowers for my office?"

"You're the Headmaster, aren't you?"

"Yes!"

"You want to win the *Golden Stick of Chalk Award* for the most efficient school in the land, don't you?"

"Yes!"

"Then take the money! Buy plants and flowers for your office. The judges have got to be impressed. We are going to win the *Golden Stick of Chalk Award.*"

With trembling hands, Old Dipstick turned the School Fund piggy bank on its back. He unscrewed the stopper from the piggy bank's tummy. Then he tipped out all the money on his desk. He looked sheepishly about him.

"Don't worry, Norman," said Mrs Belcher. "Only you and I know."

Which goes to show just how wrong you can be, even when you're Chair of the School Governors *and* Ashley Belcher's mum. For, disappearing through the wall, was the ghostly figure of Aunt Boomerang.

And Aunt Boomerang had heard everything.

Aunt Boomerang reappeared at Meryl's side. Sebastian had stopped riding and was sitting down. Or, more accurately, he had fallen off his bike and was lying on the ground with his bike on top of him.

He looked guiltily up at Aunt Boomerang as she and Meryl approached.

"Merry's told me everything, sweetheart."

Sebastian scowled at Meryl.

"I'm mighty glad she did. You're going to need all the help you can get."

There was a sudden parp-parp from a two-tone horn. Ashley sped past on his mountain bike. "Get off and milk it!" he yelled.

Aunt Boomerang stared down the road after him and concentrated. Then, for just a couple of seconds, Ashley's mountain bike turned in a toddler's trike. Ashley just managed to stay on.

"You wait 'til tomorrow!" he called back over his shoulder.

"Wow!" said Meryl.

"A skill I learnt from my time with native Australians in the outback, sweethearts," beamed Aunt Boomerang.

"Can't you turn Ashley's bike into a toddler's trike *for ever*," asked Sebastian sadly.

"Afraid not, sweetheart," sighed Aunt Boomerang. "It was fun, but you've got to win that race. And the best way to do that is to begin an intensive bike race training programme straightaway!"

Sebastian wobbled gingerly down the hill towards the woods at the bottom. He put on his brakes - not that he really needed to.

Meryl clicked the stop watch off.

"Time?" asked Aunt Boomerang fiercely.

"Ten minutes fifteen seconds," replied Meryl.

Aunt Boomerang looked impressed. "Ten minutes fifteen seconds to get from home?"

Meryl shook her head sadly. "Ten minutes fifteen seconds to get from the top of the hill to the bottom."

Aunt Boomerang sighed. "Bang goes Plan A. There's nothing else for it. I'll just have to implement Plan B."

"What's Plan B, Aunt Boomerang?" asked Meryl.

"No idea, sweetheart. I haven't thought of it yet," said Aunt Boomerang.

"I've been really stupid, haven't I?" said Sebastian quietly.

"Yes," agreed Meryl.

"Yes," agreed Aunt Boomerang.

Sebastian took the billabong blaster from his pocket. "I may never, ever see this again after Monday."

"No," agreed Meryl.

"No," agreed Aunt Boomerang. She smiled at Sebastian. "Oh, everyone does stupid things from time to time. Why look at *Cobblers.*" *Cobblers* was the Australian soap opera Aunt Boomerang had starred in when she had been alive. In fact, it was while she was on set that a sign had fallen on her head and killed her outright, which was how she had become a ghost.

"... Episode Eighty nine it was," Aunt Boomerang was saying. "Chaylene Skinner went for a swim in the forbidden Crushed Bone Creek ... very stupid of her."

"What happened to her?" asked Sebastian, though he had already guessed.

"She got stuck in the mud and was eaten alive by the crocs," said Aunt Boomerang with some relish.

Sebastian gulped. "I'm not going to race Ashley. There's no point. He's going to win anyway. I might as well just give him the billabong blaster!"

"Blistering bush babies! Mud!"

"Aunt Boomerang?"

"Mud! That's it! Plan B! Sebastian, you're going to race Ashley - and you're going to win!"

"No, Aunt Boomerang!"

"Yes!"

"No!"

Aunt Boomerang stared at Sebastian right between the eyes. "You are going to race Ashley Belcher. You are a dare-devil. What are you?"

"Er ... a daredevil," said Sebastian. "I think ...," he added doubtfully.

On Monday afternoon, the school playing field was deserted. Old Dipstick had banned games until after the *Golden Stick of Chalk Award* judges had made their visit. He wanted the playing field to look like a bowling green. He didn't want it churned up by fifty pairs of football boots.

So nobody saw the ghostly figure standing on the edge of the field holding a hose pipe. Aunt Boomerang was watering the field just a few metres from the finishing line of the bike race. She watered right through the afternoon, until there was a patch of grass that oozed and bubbled like a soggy sponge.

After school, Sebastian followed Ashley up to the park. The two of them couldn't have looked more dissimilar. A cocky-looking Ashley sat astride his mountain bike, dressed in splendid fluorescent purple and orange lycra shorts. He wore a brand new racing cyclist's crash helmet. A miserable-looking Sebastian wobbled in the saddle of his old bike, dressed in his football shorts, a Batman tee-shirt and Meryl's mum's old black velvet horse riding hat.

"Twice round the park, then down to the school and round the playing field. When I cross the finishing line first ... I get your flute thing," Ashley chuckled nastily.

Sebastian nodded sadly. Whatever Aunt Boomerang's Plan B was, there was no way it could stop Ashley Belcher beating him in a bike race.

"Ready?"

Sebastian nodded.

"After three. One, two … !"

Like the numero uno ugly brute and bully that he was, Ashley sped off without saying three and by the time he got his foot on the pedal, Sebastian was already ten metres behind.

Sebastian and Ashley's class formed two ragged lines each side of the finishing tape. On one side of the tape, Ashley's henchmen, the twins Rozza and Nozza, looked excited. On the other side of the tape, Meryl looked forlorn.

"Oh dear," she sighed. She looked down. And stayed looking down. "This bit's like a mud bath!" she said to herself.

"Of course it is, sweetheart!"

Meryl spun round and found herself facing a beaming Aunt Boomerang. "Plan B, remember?" she whispered and put her fingers to her lips.

Ashley's helmeted head was right down over the handlebars as he came to the top of the hill. He kept his head down as he began his descent. He touched his brakes lightly. But nothing happened.

"Aargh!"

At the bottom of the hill, he turned back to see Sebastian

racing down the hill behind him. *His* brakes weren't working either.

"Aargh!"

"I don't believe it!" fumed Ashley. He pedalled off towards the playing fields, Sebastian following close behind.

"Did you fix Ashley's brakes, Nozza?" asked Rozza, waiting with his brother by the finishing line.

"Aye, did you fix Sebastian's?"

"Aye." And they laughed a conspiratorial laugh.

A huge cheer went up as Ashley raced onto the field followed by a fast, free-wheeling Sebastian. Apart from Rozza and Nozza, everyone was cheering for Sebastian.

Aunt Boomerang was the only one without a smile on her face. "If Sebastian gets to the mud bath first, Plan B is doomed!" she wailed.

It was at this precise moment that Mrs Belcher got out of her car in the staff car park. She saw - and heard - the bike race spectators and was filled with disgust. She raced into Old Dipstick's office without even knocking.

"Norman! There are *children* on the playing field!"

Old Dipstick's cheeks turned the colour of his greying hair. "Children? Children? Children are trouble! And I don't like trouble!"

"I don't like trouble either," snapped Mrs Belcher.

"Especially when the *Golden Stick of Chalk Award* judges are due any minute!"

Old Dipstick was at the window. He could see a smart car pulling up. "They're here, Margaret! Quick, you see to the judges; I'll deal with those children!"

Ashley was in front and making for the finishing lines.

"No brakes!" he yelled. "Can't stop!"

Which goes to show just how wrong you can be. Even when you're wearing lycra shorts and a racing cyclist's crash helmet. For Ashley did stop. Spectacularly. The very moment his front wheel hit Aunt Boomerang's mud bath. Or rather, his bike stopped. Ashley carried on. Through the air, over his handlebars and straight into the wettest, muddiest part of the mud.

A few metres behind, Sebastian was just in time to swerve out of Ashley's way. Sending the gathered spectators flying, he skirted the mud bath, crossed the finishing line and ... carried on.

"You! Pumpkins! Stop!" yelled Old Dipstick on his way out of the school.

But, of course, Sebastian couldn't stop.

"You boy, are trouble!" bellowed Old Dipstick. "And I don't like trouble!" He didn't see Ashley, who was rising from the mud like the swamp monster. He saw Ashley's bike, though. He leapt onto the saddle and set off after Sebastian.

It took Meryl about three seconds to work out the importance of what had just happened. "Sebby's won! He crossed the finishing line before Ashley!" And she led her cheering classmates and a startled Aunt Boomerang away to find Sebastian.

Sebastian was in the privet bush that ran along the outside of the school building. Although, unless you were particularly familiar with his feet, you would probably not have known it was Sebastian, because he had ridden into the bush head first.

Old Dipstick raced up after him on Ashley's bike. He slammed on the brakes. Nothing happened.

"Aargh!" screamed Old Dipstick as, looming in front of him, behind the privet hedge, he saw the shining glass of his office window . "Aargh!"

The bike crashed into the privet hedge, catapulting Old Dipstick into the air, through his office window, across his desk and onto the floor.

Slightly dazed, he looked up. Staring down at him in a mixture of horror and alarm were Mrs Belcher and the judges of the *Golden Stick of Chalk Award*. He staggered to his feet and held out a muddy hand.

"Norman Diplock, Headmaster," he stammered. But the judges were already on their way out.

By now, Meryl and a couple of classmates had hauled

Sebastian from the privet bush, cheering and congratulating him on a his triumphant win. As the judges' car disappeared up the drive, Old Dipstick came charging out.

"You!" he bellowed to Sebastian, his voice strangely high-pitched. "Come here!"

The crowd around Sebastian fell silent. He started to walk towards Old Dipstick. Suddenly, Aunt Boomerang stepped out in front of him.

"If I might have a couple of words, Headmaster," she smiled good-naturedly.

Old Dipstick's eyes glowed in their sockets.

"You ...! Again!" he hissed. "Get off my school drive!"

Aunt Boomerang ignored him. "And the two words are ... *School Fund*," she whispered.

Old Dipstick's eyes started twitching. He turned to Mrs Belcher, who had just appeared. Aunt Boomerang saw her and gave her a cheery wave.

"Margaret!" called Old Dipstick, following her back into the school. He turned back to Sebastian.

"Out of my sight, boy!"

Aunt Boomerang, Meryl and Sebastian wandered back towards Tannochbrae Close.

"You must have some really amazing ghostly powers to make Old Dipstick change his mind like that," said Sebastian.

"Nothing to do with powers, but everything to do with *information*," smiled Aunt Boomerang.

"I was so afraid I was going to lose the billabong blaster,

Aunt Boomerang." Sebastian took it from his pocket.

Then Aunt Boomerang took a billabong blaster from *her* pocket.

"Actually, this is the real billabong blaster. I took it from your pocket and swapped it with a dud before the race. Knowing the way you ride a bike, sweetheart, I was leaving nothing to chance!"

Meryl laughed.

"So, it's goodbye big head now, is it?" Aunt Boomerang asked Sebastian. "No more stupid bets with Ashley Belcher?"

"No more stupid bets with Ashley ... " Sebastian thought for a moment. "Though I did ride a brilliant race back there. I'm sure I could beat him again – "

"Sebby!" yelled Meryl. "I've a good mind to shove your head through your front wheel!"

Sebastian grinned. "Only joking," he said.

Old Dipstick sat in his office.

"It's that Pumpkins boy."

"Simpkins," said Mrs Belcher.

"His Aunt ... It's all down to her! She's humiliated me! Again!" He looked across his desk at Mrs Belcher. There was a mad, determined look in his eye. "I'm going to get her. She's trouble, and I don't like trouble!"

Chapter 3

AN INSPECTOR CALLS

3

An Inspector Calls

"She's trouble! And I don't like trouble!" Old Dipstick marched along the school corridor, head was full of nasty thoughts about Aunt Boomerang.

Suddenly, his head began to empty of nasty thoughts about Aunt Boomerang and began, instead, to fill with the sounds of *singing*. Old Dipstick shivered and covered his ears in horror.

"I don't believe it!" he muttered to himself in disgust. "Children, somewhere in *my* school, *singing*?"

Of course, to normal ears, there is nothing quite so joyful as the sound of children singing. But Old Dipstick's were not normal ears. They were attached to the skull of the most sour and miserable head teacher in the history of sour and miserable head teachers. Old Dipstick would have preferred to listen to a class of children scraping their fingernails down a blackboard.

He strode purposefully in the direction of the offending sound. There was no doubt about it. It was Ms Goodbody's class who were singing. Suddenly, Old Dipstick did a curious thing: he smiled. A bitter, twisted sort of smile, it has to be said, but a smile, nonetheless.

He flung open the door to Ms Goodbody's classroom. "Muzz Goodbody!" he announced.

The singing petered out as the class - and Ms Goodbody - turned to see their head teacher standing in the doorway.

"Yes, Mr Diplock?" asked Ms Goodbody.

"Muzz Goodbody," Old Dipstick smiled menacingly, "it is Friday. To be precise, it is two minutes past ten on Friday morning!" He laughed crazily. "At two minutes past ten on a Friday morning, the whole of my school has a spelling test!"

"But Mr Diplock ... " began Ms Goodbody.

Old Dipstick didn't seem to hear her. "Ha. Ha. Don't worry. You sit down and rest your legs, Muzz Goodbody. I will conduct your class's spelling test for you."

He ushered Ms Goodbody to a chair in the corner.

"Gwendolen!" he cried.

With a fearful start, Meryl realised that Old Dipstick was looking at *her*.

"Me, sir?"

"There's no one else in the class called Gwendolen, is there?" asked Old Dipstick sarcastically.

"Er ... actually, my name's Meryl, Sir," said Meryl with some justification.

But Old Dipstick heard not a word. "First word. *Scream!*" he barked. "Go on!"

"Aaaarrrgghhhhh!" screamed Meryl.

Thirty one bottoms - one of which was Ms Goodbody's - leapt from their seats.

"No!!" roared Old Dipstick. "I meant spell 'scream', you dunderhead!"

Meryl blushed. "S-C-R-E-A-M-Y-O-U-D-U-N -" she began.

"That is enough!" interrupted Old Dipstick. He laughed. His left eye twitched. He laughed some more. His right eye twitched. "Muzz Goodbody," he said, "see me in my office straight after school!"

At three thirty one precisely, Ms Goodbody stood in front of Old Dipstick's desk. Sitting next to Old Dipstick was Mrs Belcher. Mrs Belcher smiled - a sinister, leering smile that could have curdled a pot of cream at twenty paces.

"Mrs Belcher and I have been discussing certain activities that you have been involved with," Old Dipstick began. "Like the five-a-side football competition - "

" - Which my little Ashley's team should've won!" interrupted Mrs Belcher vehemently.

"This morning's fiasco was the last straw," Old Dipstick went on.

"You mean the singing lesson?" asked Ms Goodbody.

"Of course I mean the singing lesson," hissed Old Dipstick. "Singing is not useful!"

"Oh, it is - " protested Ms Goodbody.

"For kettles maybe," spluttered Old Dipstick, "but not for children! We have an inspector visiting the school next week and I want him to see a school that is ordered and disciplined, where children are learning the three S's - Spelling, Spelling and er ... Some-More-Spelling. You are on a temporary contract, Muzz Goodbody. That contract is now terminated. You will collect your things from your classroom. You will not return to school on Monday."

Ms Goodbody looked close to tears. "But Mr Diplock," she protested, "you can't! I've grown fond of this school. And I really like the children - "

"Teachers are paid to *teach* children, not to *like* them, Ms Goodbody," said Mrs Belcher acidly.

"How will you get another teacher by Monday?" asked Ms Goodbody.

Old Dipstick laughed madly. "Who said anything about another teacher? Teachers are trouble." He sneered unpleasantly at Ms Goodbody. "And I don't like trouble."

"Cor, look!" exclaimed Sebastian excitedly as he and Meryl walked into class the following Monday morning. Well might he have said "Cor, look", for two giant TV monitors hung from the ceiling at the front of the classroom.

"We're going to watch telly all day!"

The class quickly settled down.

"Where's Ms Goodbody?" asked Meryl with a frown.

"Dunno," said Sebastian.

Suddenly the TV monitors flickered into life and thirty open mouths gasped in horror as Old Dipstick's leering face filled both giant screens.

"Good morning, children!" said Old Dipstick brightly. "As you can see, Muzz Goodbody has been replaced as your class teacher by a Closed Circuit TV System."

Slowly, as Old Dipstick droned on, the full horror of the situation began to sink in.

" ...The work you are to undertake during the day," Old Dipstick continued, "will appear on the screens. Starting with your 138 times table which you are all to learn by lunchtime."

Old Dipstick's face disappeared briefly from the screens to be replaced by two columns of the 138 times table. There was worse to come.

"There will, of course, need to be a responsible member of class to ensure that the monitor in your classroom is not switched off." Old Dipstick sneered. "Ashley Belcher, I appoint you class monitor-monitor!"

"Ye-eh!" roared Ashley.

The rest of the class didn't respond. They were still too numb with shock to be able to move even the smallest muscle in their faces.

"Nice day at school, you two?" asked Mrs Simpkins dreamily. She had a drill in one hand and a saw in the other. A wooden bed frame was propped against the sink. Sebastian and Meryl weren't surprised. Unable to cope with any more of her husband's DIY disasters, Mrs Simpkins had taken up DIY herself. Mr Simpkins had taken over Mrs Simpkins' potter's wheel and kiln.

"We had to learn our 138 times table," muttered Sebastian.

"That's nice, dear."

"Where's Aunt Boomerang?"

"Out," said Mrs Simpkins. "That's why I thought I'd crack on with this. It's a luxury bed for her." She smiled. "I mean, what with her being a famous Australian soap star and all, you can't expect her to sleep on that lumpy old thing we got from Beds R Us can you?"

Sebastian and Meryl mooched off down to the park. They sat on the swings and looked up at the trees, fully expecting a giant TV monitor with Old Dipstick's face on it to appear from the branches.

Sebastian took the billabong blaster from his pocket and blew hard. There was a sudden whoosh behind them.

"Strewth! I think I've ripped my chemise!" cried a familiar voice.

Sebastian and Meryl turned around just in time to see Aunt Boomerang drifting out of a hawthorn hedge.

"G'day, sweethearts! High Noon?"

Sebastian and Meryl told Aunt Boomerang the dreadful news.

"He's done *what*?!" she exploded.

"Sacked Ms Goodbody!"

"He's replaced her with *what*?"

"A closed circuit TV!"

"He's made Ashley Belcher *what*?"

"The monitor-monitor!"

Aunt Boomerang snorted crossly. "Things must be put right," she said firmly. "Justice must be done!"

"Perhaps you should have a word with Old Dipstick," suggested Meryl. "You're a grown-up. He might listen to you."

"I doubt it, sweetheart. He already thinks it was me who shrunk his referee's kit and sabotaged the bike race."

"Aunt Boomerang, it *was* you who shrunk his ref's kit and sabotaged the bike race," reasoned Sebastian.

"A fair point," admitted Aunt Boomerang.

"Oh dear," sighed Meryl.

"You say there's a school inspector visiting?"

"Tomorrow."

"Then this calls for Plan B!" declared Aunt Boomerang.

"Is this Plan B going to be messy?" asked Sebastian, his mind going back to Aunt Boomerang's last Plan B which had involved turning the school playing field into a mud bath.

"I couldn't be a hundred per cent sure - I haven't thought of it yet," smiled Aunt Boomerang. "But, as a general rule, sweetheart, Plan B's are very messy indeed."

"Oh good," said Sebastian.

It was midnight. The witching hour. Meryl slept soundly. She didn't hear the faint whoosh as a ghostly figure stepped through her bedroom wall. She did hear the crash as her in-line skates were knocked off her dressing table, though. She sat up in bed with a start.

"It's all right, sweetheart," whispered a familiar voice.

"Aunt Boomerang?"

"Sorry about your skates. Hope I haven't woken your mum and grandad."

"My grandad's deaf and if my mum hears noises she thinks it's my grandad anyway. He plays darts in his bed-room," Meryl explained.

"At two o'clock in the morning?"

"Oh yes."

"Plan B," smiled Aunt Boomerang triumphantly. "I've worked it out."

Meryl frowned. "But why have you come to tell me - at two o'clock in the morning?"

"Because, sweetheart, you are central to the success of Plan B," smiled Aunt Boomerang.

"Really?" said Meryl excitedly. "What have I got to do?"

"Sing," said Aunt Boomerang.

"Sing?"

"In front of the school inspector and Old Dipstick. And this is the song ... " Aunt Boomerang thrust a sheet of paper into Meryl's hands. "I wrote it myself," she added proudly.

Meryl cast her eyes over the lyrics. "I can't sing *that*," cried a panic-stricken Meryl. "Old Dipstick will kill me! Can't *you* sing it? You wrote it."

Aunt Boomerang looked stern. "Merry," she said. "You - and the rest of your class - have a problem. A big problem. Now, I can use my powers to help you, but I can't be the one that actually puts things right. That has to be you."

"Can't Sebby sing it?"

"Have you ever heard Sebastian sing?"

Meryl nodded sadly.

"There's your answer then. The sound of Sebastian singing solo would probably break every window in the school."

"Oh dear," sighed Meryl gloomily.

Aunt Boomerang looked straight into Meryl's eyes and held them there. "I turn scaredy-cats into daredevils. You can do it, sweetheart. You can do it."

Moonlight cast a greyish glow around the walls of Old Dipstick's office. There was a whoosh as a familiar ghostly figure walked in through the window. A long white finger flicked on the computer that was attached to the closed circuit TV system.

On the screen appeared a list of work for Sebastian's class. "Levers and Pulleys" was the title. A page of instructions followed.

"Bonza!" cried the ghostly figure. Once again, a long white finger stretched out and silently hit the "Delete" key. All that remained on the screen were the words "Levers and Pulleys". The ghostly fingers began to type. The ghostly voice began to chuckle.

Moonlight also cast a greyish glow over the school kitchen. A ghostly hand began opening cupboard doors and then closing them.

"Bonza!" said a ghostly voice eventually, as two ghostly hands took down a bag of flour.

Ten minutes later, the bag of flour was on Ms Goodbody's desk.

Ms Goodbody's breakfast of carrot juice and chocolate fudge cake was interrupted by a frantic ringing at her front door bell.

"All right, all right!" she called.

She opened the door and found herself face-to-face with a pale woman of uncertain age, dressed in a long black frock and flowing red velvet gown.

"My goodness," Ms Goodbody exclaimed in a startled voice. "Aunt Boomerang!"

"G'day, sweetheart," beamed Aunt Boomerang. "Grab your tucker bag and get moving. We're going to Millstone School."

"I've been sacked from Millstone School," replied Ms Goodbody tartly.

"That's why we're going there, sweetheart. To get you unsacked. Where's your car?"

"I haven't got a car," said Ms Goodbody.

"Then what have you got?" asked Aunt Boomerang.

"A bike."

"A bike!" exclaimed Aunt Boomerang despairingly. "Strewth, I hope it's fast."

"The fastest there is," answered Ms Goodbody with a wry smile. And she nodded towards the side path where, perched on its stand, stood 1000cc's worth of gleaming Harley Davidson motorbike.

The school inspector didn't much like schools. He liked inspecting them even less. He wanted to get the inspection of Millstone School over and done with. He wanted to get home to the real passion in his life: his priceless collection of Patagonian Dung Beetles. As he walked down the school corridor with Old Dipstick and Mrs Belcher, he stifled a yawn.

In contrast, Old Dipstick was all excitement. He waved his arms about and his left eye twitched as he spoke.

"You know, until I installed this closed circuit TV, I had nothing but trouble with these children."

The school inspector stifled another yawn.

"And their teacher," added Mrs Belcher bitterly.

"I don't like trouble," explained Old Dipstick.

As the door opened, Ms Goodbody's class rose to their feet as one. "Good morning, Mr Diplock! Good morning, School Inspector! Er ... good morning, Ashley's mum!" they chorused in unison.

"Sit!" commanded Old Dipstick as if he were addressing a pack of particularly troublesome dogs.

The class sat.

Old Dipstick turned to the school inspector. "As I explained," he said, "this class has been learning about levers_ and pulleys from our wonderful computerised closed circuit TV. Now, I wonder who can give us a practical demonstration of what has been learnt?"

Ashley's hand shot up. His mum was quick to see it. She nudged Old Dipstick.

"Ah ... yes ... Ashley! Ashley is the class monitor-monitor," he explained to the school inspector.

Ashley smirked at the rest of the class, then walked up to a model see-saw on the front desk and cleared his throat and began to read from the TV monitor.

"This model will demonstrate the lever principle. First, you take a fistful of flour ... "

Old Dipstick's eyes bolted from their sockets in alarm as Ashley took a fistful of flour from the bag on the desk.

" ... then you roll it into a ball with some water and place it on the lever ... "

Ashley rolled it into ball with some water and placed it on the lever.

Old Dipstick stared open-mouthed at the screen, struggling to understand how his instructions had been suddenly changed. The school inspector stared open-mouthed at Old Dipstick. Mrs Belcher stared open-mouthed at Ashley.

"Then, you strike the other end of the lever," Ashley read from the screen.

"Stop!" squeaked Old Dipstick in a terrified voice. But too late.

Ashley struck the other end of the see-saw lever. The flour ball flew swiftly through the air. It landed with a satisfying plop straight into Old Dipstick's twitching left eye.

"Aargh!" cried Old Dipstick.

The class struggled to hide their laughter behind their hands.

"Well, I never!" gasped a startled school inspector.

"Ashley!" exclaimed a horrified Mrs Belcher.

"Ashley!" hissed a seething Old Dipstick.

"I followed the instructions," whined the pathetic Ashley.

The class were finding it difficult to control their laughter. Until ...

"Quiet, everyone!" ordered a firm, unruffled voice. Thirty three faces turned to see Ms Goodbody standing in the doorway.

Ms Goodbody marched straight up to the school inspector and shook his hand.

"I am Sabrina Goodbody," she told him. "I taught this class." Here she cast a dangerous look at Old Dipstick who was cowering in the corner, "Until last Friday."

Ms Goodbody glanced towards the doorway and caught the briefest of glimpses of Aunt Boomerang clenching her fists in encouragement. She took a deep breath.

"Perhaps you'd like a demonstration of something the class learnt with me?" she asked the school inspector, none too confidently.

"Huh!" growled Old Dipstick, wiping flour from his eye.

"Does it involve flour bombs?" asked the school inspector, intrigued.

"Certainly not!" said Ms Goodbody. "It involves, er ... a song."

"Huh!" growled Old Dipstick again.

Ms Goodbody continued, still with doubt in her voice, "And Meryl will sing it for us."

Meryl stood up. She caught sight of Aunt Boomerang standing behind Ms Goodbody, Mrs Belcher, Old Dipstick and the school inspector. She felt the strength of Aunt Boomerang's smile. She opened her mouth and sang.

"Our lovely school has dead strict rules:
'No swearing' and 'No lipstick'.
And at its helm's a bonza man,
Our wondrous head Old Dipstick, ... er, Mr Diplock.

And what a privilege 'tis today,
To see the School Inspector.
He's wise and knowing, handsome,too
Not at all like Hannibal Lecter.

We learn our spellings and our sums,
Our geometry and our grammar,
So when we leave,we'll all get jobs
And not end up in the slammer."

It was the school inspector who led the cheering and applause. Eventually, he raised his hand for silence.

"A fine song, expressing fine sentiments!" he said.

He turned to Old Dipstick. "Mr Diplock, in the circumstances, I must instruct you to remove this ... this ... ," he waved a dismissive hand at the TV monitors, " ... technological junk and reinstate Ms Goodbody to her rightful place as class teacher immediately!"

"Bonza!" yelled a jubilant voice. Not everyone saw Aunt Boomerang disappear quickly through the door, but Old Dipstick did.

The whole class, with the exception of Ashley of course , was cheering. Ms Goodbody smiled radiantly as the class swarmed round a blushing, but triumphant Meryl.

Back in his office, Old Dipstick wiped flour and water from his face.

"Well, Norman," Mrs Belcher hissed threateningly at Old Dipstick. "What are you going to do now?"

"I am going to get her!" muttered Old Dipstick, his face all a rage.

"Get who?" asked Mrs Belcher.

"Who do you think?" retorted Old Dipstick. "The barmy Aunt Boobybang person! She's responsible for this! I know it!""

Aunt Boomerang sat at the kitchen table with Meryl and Sebastian. They tried to make each other heard above the sounds of drilling and hammering coming from Aunt Boomerang's room above. The noise stopped.

"Thanks for sorting it all out, Aunt Boomerang," said Sebastian.

Aunt Boomerang shrugged modestly. "It was Merry who sang the song."

The kitchen door crashed open and Mrs Simpkins stood there, grinning excitedly. "I've finished the special bed I was making for you, Aunt Boomerang!"

"What are we waiting for? Let's go and have a look!" declared Aunt Boomerang.

They had just reached the top of the stairs, when they were stopped in their tracks by a furious hammering on the front door. Mrs Simpkins went down to investigate. On the doorstep stood Old Dipstick.

"Where is she? That Aunt Bangyboom woman?"

"Mr Dipstick - er ... lock!" called Aunt Boomerang from the top of the stairs. "Won't you come up?"

Old Dipstick needed no second bidding. He charged into the hall and up the stairs past a startled Mrs Simpkins.

He followed Aunt Boomerang into her room. Sebastian and Meryl stood there horrified, but Old Dipstick didn't have eyes for them. He glowered at Aunt Boomerang. "Once again, woman, you have made me look a fool!"

"It doesn't need me to do that, Mr Diplock," shrugged Aunt Boomerang with a sigh.

Old Dipstick's nostrils twitched. "Ever since your arrival in this town," he went on, "you've caused nothing but trouble. And I don't like trouble!"

Old Dipstick was waving his arms in fury. As he did so, he knocked a lever at the side of Aunt Boomerang's new bed. The foot of the bed began to rise up towards the wall. It caught Old Dipstick behind the knees. His legs gave way beneath him and he fell back on the bed.

"Aargh!" cried Old Dipstick as the bed swung back to the wall with a gentle thud.

Sticking out of the side of the bed were two hands and two feet.

Aunt Boomerang, Mrs Simpkins, Sebastian and Meryl - watched the proceedings with fascination and horror. It was difficult for them to actually hear what Old Dipstick was trying to say from behind thirty centimetres of spring interior mattress. At a guess, though, they would have said that it sounded something like, "Aunt Bongybum, you're nothing but trouble! And I don't like trouble! I'm going to get you! Oh yes, I'm going to get you!"

Chapter 4

ON THE RUN

4

On The Run

"Aunt Bongybum, you're nothing but trouble! And I don't like trouble! I'm going to get you! Oh yes, I'm going to get you!' Old Dipstick crouched behind a wheelie bin in Tannochbrae Close and trained his binoculars on the door of Number 40.

"Correction, Norman," hissed Mrs Belcher, who was crouched beside Old Dipstick. "*We're* going to get her!"

Sounds of drilling filled the Simpkins' house. Sebastian, making his way upstairs, detected the source of the noise as coming from Aunt Boomerang's room. He poked his head through her open door, but the room seemed to be empty. Suddenly, the sound of drilling stopped. Then, slowly, Aunt Boomerang's wardrobe door opened. Sebastian's mum appeared. She was holding an electric drill.

"I'm building Aunt Boomerang a shower," said Sebastian's mum.

"In the *wardrobe*?"

"In the wardrobe."

"Nice," said Sebastian doubtfully. He sighed. "Mum.

What about Sunday lunch?"

Mrs Simpkins clapped her hand over her mouth in surprise. "Oh Sebastian ... I didn't realise ... "

"You didn't realise it was lunchtime?" Sebastian asked incredulously.

Mrs Simpkins frowned. "No, I didn't realise it was Sunday!"

Sebastian lay on his bed and shook his head in despair. He took the billabong blaster from his pocket. He frowned. Was this an emergency? Of course it was! If he didn't eat soon, he would face a long and lingering death from starvation. He blew hard on the billabong blaster. There was a whoosh and a familiar figure appeared through the window and drifted to the end of his bed.

"G'day, sweetheart! High Noon?"

"Not High Noon exactly," admitted Sebastian. "Just, er ... noon Noon."

Aunt Boomerang eyed Sebastian suspiciously. "What do you mean, sweetheart?"

"I mean, I'm hungry and Mum's forgotten to cook lunch!"

Aunt Boomerang bridled. "Sweetheart," she said, stiffly, "I am the ghost of an Australian soap star. I am not Dial-a-Pizza!"

"But I could starve to death!" protested Sebastian.

Before Aunt Boomerang could reply, the sound of door

chimes filled the air. But not just any old door chimes. Door chimes that were playing the theme tune from *Neighbours*. Aunt Boomerang covered her ears with her hands.

"Woggling wallabies, *what* is that?"

Aunt Boomerang disappeared through the door - literally. Sebastian raced after her, remembering, just in time, that he needed to open the door to get through it.

On the front doorstep stood Meryl, her hand pressed firmly on the door bell in dazzled fascination.

"No!" cried Aunt Boomerang. "Merry, sweetheart, if you have any compassion, stop it!"

Meryl took her hand off the door bell.

"Don't you like them, Aunt Boomerang?"

"Mum put them in," explained Sebastian. "She thought they'd make you feel at home."

"Sebastian," sighed Aunt Boomerang, " I am the ghost of an Australian soap star who spent twelve years working on the Australian soap, *Cobblers*. Now, *Cobblers* is to *Neighbours* what Man U is to Crewe Alexandra. Do I make myself clear?"

"Can I come in?" asked Meryl. "Your mum invited me for Sunday lunch, remember?"

"*I* remember," sighed Sebastian, "but *she* doesn't. She doesn't even remember it's Sunday."

"Come on," said Aunt Boomerang. "I'll treat you all to lunch at The White Heather Cafe."

The White Heather Cafe nestled in the middle of a row of small shops just off the main road. It was Aunt Boomerang's favourite restaurant. She adored their kippers. Being a ghost, she didn't eat them, of course. But, like all ghosts, she had an amazing sense of smell. There was nothing she liked more than the aroma of freshly grilled kippers.

Sebastian and Meryl tucked into all-day breakfasts. Aunt Boomerang sniffed a plate of kippers.

"Did you know Mum's building you a shower in your wardrobe?" Sebastian asked Aunt Boomerang through a mouthful of fried egg.

"Yes," nodded Aunt Boomerang. "I did think of telling her that I don't ever wash, but I didn't think she'd take it the right way. You see, she wants to impress me, so that I'll get her on the TV."

"Oh no, she'd be so embarrassing," sighed Sebastian.

"Don't worry, sweetheart, what can I do to get her on the TV? I'm dead, remember?" smiled Aunt Boomerang. "Come on, cheer up! It's Sunday and it's half term. No school. No Old Dipstick watching you."

Which goes to show just how wrong you can be, even when you're the ghost of an Australian soap star. For, at that very moment, Old Dipstick and Mrs Belcher were watching Meryl, Sebastian and Aunt Boomerang through the window of The White Heather Cafe.

"What can you see, Norman?" whispered Mrs Belcher.

"What are they hatching in there?"

Old Dipstick felt his stomach rumble. He was hungry. He watched Sebastian tucking into his all-day breakfast.

"Eggs!" he said wistfully.

Old Dipstick and Mrs Belcher crept into The White Heather Cafe. They found a table behind a pair of French and Scottish flags, from where - unseen - they could hear Aunt Boomerang, Sebastian and Meryl talking.

Aunt Boomerang shivered. "Blistering bushbabies."

"What's wrong, Aunt Boomerang?" asked Sebastian.

"I'm sensing a bad aura," said Aunt Boomerang with a frown.

"Oh dear," sighed Meryl. "Perhaps it's your kippers."

"No," said Aunt Boomerang, seriously. "I mean vibes. Ugly, unpleasant vibes."

"Don't worry about it, Aunt Boomerang," shrugged Sebastian.

"Oh, but I do, sweetheart, I do," replied Aunt Boomerang quickly. "One of the reasons I came over to Scotland is that the episodes of *Cobblers* on your TV screens are five years behind those in Australia."

Sebastian had stopped eating. He looked up with concern into Aunt Boomerang's face. "What do you mean?"

"I mean that people here don't know that the actress who played Aunt Boomerang died four years ago." Aunt

Boomerang was bending close to Meryl and Sebastian and talking quietly; not quietly enough, though, to prevent Mrs Belcher and Old Dipstick from overhearing.

Mrs Belcher grabbed Old Dipstick's arm in excitement. Startled, Old Dipstick's elbow slipped from the tartan table-cloth and his face dropped straight into a plate of leftover mash and gravy.

"Come on," hissed Mrs Belcher. And she hauled Old Dipstick - his face dripping gravy - out of the White Heather Cafe.

Aunt Boomerang, Meryl and Sebastian, huddled together over their table, neither heard nor saw any of this.

"How did you die?" Sebastian asked Aunt Boomerang. Even as he said it, he knew it sounded a weird question, but he felt deep down he needed to know the answer.

"It was on set," said Aunt Boomerang. "A boom mike caught the giant *Cobblers* shop sign which fell off its hooks - straight onto my head."

"But why did you come back as the ghost of your TV character and not as yourself?" asked Meryl.

Aunt Boomerang shrugged. "I don't really think I had a choice sweetheart. I had become my TV character. When people stopped me in the street they didn't say 'G'day, Miss Bigsby - which was my real name. They said 'G'day, Aunt Boomerang!' All the letters I ever got were addressed, not to Miss Celia Bigsby, but to Aunt Boomerang. The public thought I was Aunt Boomerang ... and so, in the end, did I. I stopped being Celia Bigsby and became Aunt Boomerang." She paused and sighed sadly. "Perhaps I even liked my TV character better than I did my real self. Anyway, when I died and became a ghost, I had no choice but to return to earth as Aunt Boomerang."

"Wow," said Meryl.

"So, if people found out that you died on set four years ago, they'd know you were a ghost," frowned Sebastian.

Aunt Boomerang shook her head. "As a rule, grown-ups don't believe in ghosts."

"So, what *would* they think you were, then?" asked Sebastian.

"An imposter and a fraud," replied Aunt Boomerang grimly.

"An imposter and a fraud! That's what she is!" Old Dipstick spluttered triumphantly through the remaining traces of gravy around his mouth. He was hopping about in mad excitement just around the corner from The White Heather Cafe.

Mrs Belcher had her mobile phone to her ear. "Hello?" she was saying. "Is that *The Scum* newspaper? I've got a story for you. No ... it's not about the Royal Family ... no, not Charlie Dimmock ... it's better than that ... it's about an Australian soap star ... Fine yes ... Good!"

Mrs Belcher grinned a nasty grin. She put the phone down and looked back towards The White Heather Cafe. Aunt Boomerang could just be seen, still talking with Sebastian and Meryl, completely unaware of the danger closing in on her.

Mrs Belcher chuckled. "Gotcha," she hissed.

Next morning, the sound of the *Neighbours* theme tune filled the Simpkins house. Someone was ringing the front door bell: incessantly, impatiently.

Mrs Simpkins opened the front door to be confronted by a furry microphone.

"Where is she?" demanded a wild-eyed young woman who was clutching the microphone.

"Where's who?" asked a startled Mrs Simpkins.

"Aunt Boomerang, of course!"

Mrs Simpkins suddenly registered the hordes of people with TV cameras standing in the front garden. She felt a frisson of excitement run through her.

"Are you a docu-soap? Or are you from *Changing Rooms*? What do you think of my chimes? They're rather nice aren't they - "

"Stuff the chimes," spat the young woman with the microphone. "It's Aunt Boomerang I want. Or rather the woman calling herself Aunt Boomerang. She's holed up here, isn't she?"

Before a flustered Mrs Simpkins could answer, Sebastian had tumbled down the stairs, raced across the hall, slammed the front door and slid the bolts.

"Tracey! Sebastian! In here, quick!" cried Mr Simpkins' voice from the kitchen.

Sebastian and Mrs Simpkins found him watching TV.

" ... And so the question posed by *The Scum* newspaper this morning remains," the man on the TV was saying. "What is the secret behind the woman who up until her death four years ago brought such painful scenes as these ... "

Onto the screen flashed a grainy picture of a hospital bed. On it lay the prostate figure completely covered in bandages. Someone was sitting on a chair next to the bed, a very familiar someone: Aunt Boomerang.

"Keithie," Aunt Boomerang was saying to the bandages, *"You mean, all the time you've been calling me Auntie, you've really been hiding the fact that you are Kayleigh, mother of my nephew Shane's love child? And yet, I see it now. You look just like a mummy ..."*

The cameras pulled back and Sebastian could see what Aunt Boomerang meant. In all those bandages, Keithie did look like a mummy - an Egyptian mummy.

The screen flashed again.

"Oh look!" exclaimed Mrs Simpkins. "There's that extremely rude reporter-girl who was at the door just now."

"Did Celia Bigsby, the actress who played *Cobblers'* barmy

Aunt Boomerang for so many years, fake her own death?" the extremely rude reporter-girl was saying. "Or is the woman hiding out in this unassuming Scottish house an imposter?"

"Oh look, it's our house!" cried Mrs Simpkins excitedly.

The camera pulled back to reveal a crowd of onlookers standing behind the extremely rude reporter-girl.

"And there's your Headmaster ... and that's Margaret Belcher, your little friend Ashley's mum, isn't it, Sebastian? Sebastian?" But Sebastian was no longer standing in the kitchen. He was upstairs, hammering for all his worth on Aunt Boomerang's bedroom door.

The door was opened, not by an Australian soap star in a red velvet gown carrying a handbag, but by an eleven year old girl in tee-shirt and jeans carrying a rope and a grappling hook.

"Meryl?" asked an astonished Sebastian.

"I couldn't get to your front door," she explained. "Your front garden's full of reporters and TV crews. Not to mention Old Dipstick and Ashley's mum. So I borrowed my brother's mountaineering gear. I climbed up the wall and in through Aunt Boomerang's window."

Aunt Boomerang was packing a large suitcase.

"Sweethearts," she said, anxiously, "I've got to go into hiding."

"But you're a ghost," protested Sebastian. "You don't need to go into hiding!"

"Sebastian," said Aunt Boomerang firmly, "do you really think I want to spend my afterlife being chased through walls by a bunch of press hoodlums? Not to mention Old Dipstick and the Belcher woman?"

Aunt Boomerang was stopped by the sound of an almighty crash from the kitchen. Someone had broken their way in through the kitchen door.

"Where is she? Where's boomy Aunt Barmyrang?" yelled a familiar voice.

"Old Dipstick!" cried Sebastian.

"Oh dear," cried Meryl.

"Get down to the kitchen and put him off the scent!" whispered Aunt Boomerang, panic stricken. "And play for time ... !"

"Me?" asked a horror-struck Sebastian.

"Me?" asked a terrified Meryl.

"Of course, you!" snorted Aunt Boomerang. "Why do you think I bother to turn scaredy-cats into daredevils?"

Old Dipstick was eyeballing a startled Mr Simpkins.

"That old Aussie woman you've got staying here is a complete and utter fraud!"

"Oh no she isn't!" replied Mr Simpkins.

"Oh yes she is!" cried Mrs Belcher, crashing in through the back door.

Mrs Simpkins decided it was time to re-establish control of her home. "Mr Diplock, Mrs Belcher, kindly leave my kitchen," she commanded.

"It's *Councillor* Belcher to you."

"Don't come that tone with me," replied Mrs Simpkins, her cheeks flushed with anger. "I remember when you and I used to be neighbours in that pokey little tenement block down McShettie Alley. It wasn't *Councillor* we called you then. It was Scraggie Maggie!"

Mrs Belcher blanched. Old Dipstick took up the cudgels on her behalf. "That barmy Aunt Bangaboom woman is a fraud and an imposter!" Old Dipstick rubbed his hands together. "Shop her and you could sell your story to *The Scum* for millions! Millions!"

"Nobody is going to shop Aunt Boomerang," said a quiet, authoritative voice from the hall doorway. Sebastian stepped into the kitchen.

Meryl followed him in. "You heard what he said," she added calmly.

"Children," hissed Old Dipstick through clenched teeth. "Nothing but trouble." He paused. "I don't like trouble!"

"Listen," said Mrs Belcher, trying, but failing utterly, to sound understanding and reasonable. "That old lady who's staying with you is ... not who she says she is."

"You're just a sour-faced old snob," said Sebastian and immediately wondered where the bare-faced cheek to say such a thing had come from.

Mrs Belcher snorted like a charging bull. She turned to Mr Simpkins. "Are you going to let your son speak to me like that?" she asked him.

"Sebastian!" said Mr Simpkins sternly. "How dare you? " He paused. "Actually, he's right. You *are* a sour-faced old snob. A *mean* sour-faced old snob."

Mrs Belcher stepped forward. As she did so, she seemed to trip. Quite how wasn't exactly clear, but Sebastian and Meryl could have sworn they saw a ghostly ankle extend itself in front of Mrs Belcher's feet. As she fell, Mrs Belcher knocked Mr Simpkins, whose foot slipped onto the potter's wheel pedal. As Mr Simpkins' foot pressed down onto the pedal, the wheel began to spin. A large dollop of wet clay flew off the wheel and all over Mrs Belcher.

"You ... you ... !" she spluttered as she backed off towards the back door covered in wet clay. She beckoned Old Dipstick to follow her. "We'll be back!" she threatened. "We'll be back!"

Outside, the TV crews and reporters gathered around Old Dipstick and Mrs Belcher, anxious for word of Aunt Boomerang's whereabouts. None of them spotted the two insignificant-looking children racing out of 40 Tannochbrae Close and off up the road.

"We'll be back," Old Dipstick was telling the reporters. "Just as soon as Mrs Belcher has got a change of clothes. Come along, Margaret!"

But Mrs Belcher didn't come. Mrs Belcher couldn't

come. The wet clay that covered Mrs Belcher from her orange hair to her purple toenails had hardened and she stood there, solid, like a giant garden gnome.

Sebastian and Meryl ran on and on, past Millstone School to a part of the city where the streets were wider and the cars were smarter.

"Are you sure this place will be all right for Aunt Boomerang to hide away in?" asked Sebastian doubtfully.

"Of course," said Meryl. "Prince Charles stays here all the time."

"Right," said Sebastian, a little more reassured.

They turned through a wide drive. Sebastian stopped, aghast. "Is this it?"

"Aye!"

"This isn't a five star hotel!" exclaimed Sebastian.

"No," agreed Meryl. " It's the allotments. And that ... " Meryl pointed to an imposing but small green wooden building, " ... is my grandad's shed."

"And that's where you think Aunt Boomerang can stay?" Meryl nodded.

"I thought you said Prince Charles stays here?"

"He does!" insisted Meryl. She paused. "Prince Charles is my grandad's whippet."

Sebastian sighed. "Oh well, we'd better see what she thinks about it, hadn't we?" He took out the billabong blaster and blew. There was a whoosh behind them – and there stood Aunt Boomerang.

She took one brief look at Meryl's grandad's shed. "It's bonza, sweethearts!"

Meryl flashed Sebastian a "told-you-so" look.

"Takes me back to the days when I used to go walkabout in the outback," said Aunt Boomerang. She was rummaging in her bag. She took out a fistful of ten pound notes and thrust them at Sebastian.

"Aunt Boomerang ... ?" said Sebastian, slightly hurt. "We don't want your money!"

"You're not getting my money!" snorted Aunt Boomerang. "*That* is for your parents." She paused. "To pay for the damage to the carpet."

"Damage to the carpet?" repeated Sebastian, mystified.

Aunt Boomerang looked a bit sheepish. "While you were making your way up here, I called on Meryl's mum and got her to pass an anonymous message on to Old Dipstick."

"What was the message?" asked Meryl.

"Try the wardrobe ... ," chortled Aunt Boomerang.

Mr and Mrs Simpkins stood in Aunt Boomerang's room. They were glancing over a note that had been left for them.

"Thanks. You've been marvellous, both of you. I've gone to spend a few weeks in the lap of luxury. Take care, your ever-loving barmy Aunt Boomerang."

Mrs Simpkins sniffed and blew her nose.

"So, if she's not an imposter, what is she?" asked Mr

Simpkins.

"She's ... barmy Aunt Boomerang," said Mrs Simpkins quietly. "That's enough, isn't it?"

Mr Simpkins nodded and smiled. "More than enough," he said.

Suddenly, there was a crash downstairs.

"Oh no!" cried Mrs Simpkins. "I didn't lock the back door!"

Before Mr and Mrs Simpkins had time to stop them, Mrs Belcher and Old Dipstick were up the stairs and in Aunt Boomerang's bedroom.

"Get out of my house!" yelled Mr Simpkins. But Mrs Belcher pushed him out of the way.

"Try the wardrobe! That's what the message said!" blubbered Old Dipstick deliriously. "She's in the wardrobe, I know it!

With a flourish, Mrs Belcher flung open Aunt Boomerang's wardrobe door. A gush of water shot forth, drenching both Old Dipstick and Mrs Belcher. Aunt Boomerang had tried Mrs Simpkins' new shower - and had left it on.

"I'm going to get her!" screamed Old Dipstick, wiping a splodge of shower gel which was bubbling from his wild eyes. "I'm going to get her! Oh yes!"

Chapter 5

A TURN UP AT
THE BURN UP

75

5

A Turn Up at the Burn Up

"I'm going to get her! Oh yes! I'm going to get her" snarled Old Dipstick. He looked up sharply. "And there's no need to stare at me like that!" There was no reply, mainly because Old Dipstick wasn't talking to another person but to a pickled onion on the end of a fork. He popped the pickled onion into his mouth and washed it down with a flask of beef tea.

He went to his office window and peered out into the playground . He didn't like what he saw, which was a dumped car left there by a gang of joyriders the night before. He looked across to the other side of the playground. What he saw there he liked even less: two hundred children running around laughing, enjoying their lunch hour break.

"Enter!" he called in response to a knock at his door.

He turned round and found Ashley Belcher standing demurely in front of his desk.

"Ah, Ashley," whined Old Dipstick. "As you know, I am not a vindictive man. Oh, no. I am quite prepared to draw a line under last week's unfortunate incident."

"You mean when I pinged a flour bomb in your eye?" enquired Ashley.

Old Dipstick's hands instinctively went straight to Ashley's throat in a throttling motion. Ashley stepped back just in time.

"I am prepared to let you go unpunished," Old Dipstick gave a mad little laugh, "providing you do a little job for me today after school."

"What job's that, sir?"

"I want you to find out where Pumpkins is hiding his barmy Aunt Bangybum. And I want you to come and tell me. She's trouble, you know!" He gave another mad little laugh. "And I don't like trouble!"

At half past three, Sebastian and Meryl turned left out of Millstone School and walked towards a part of the city where the streets were wider and the cars were smarter.

"I wonder why Old Dipstick didn't give us a detention tonight?" Sebastian asked Meryl.

"I don't know," sighed Meryl. "He said he was going to give us a detention every night and ban us from the school camp until we tell him where Aunt Boomerang is."

Sebastian nodded. "But today, he seemed almost keen to get us out of school at home time."

"Weird," agreed Meryl.

They were too deep in thought to notice a hunched, determined figure following them at a discreet distance: a figure whose face bore an evil little grin. It was the kind of evil little grin you can only manage if your name is Ashley Belcher.

At first, Meryl's grandad had been somewhat miffed to find the ghost of an Australian soap star hiding out amongst his seed potatoes and onion sets. But Aunt Boomerang had had little trouble in winning him round.

"So, you will let me stay, Wally?" Aunt Boomerang had fluttered her eye lashes at Meryl's grandad. Then she had explained how she was being pursued by the odious *Scum* newspaper and the even more odious Old Dipstick and Mrs Belcher.

Meryl's grandad had scratched his chin. "Well, so long as you're not a psychopathic axe-murderer."

"Oh, I'm not!" Aunt Boomerang had assured him.

"Or a Man U supporter?"

Aunt Boomerang had been outraged. "Most definitely not!"

And that had been that.

Now Sebastian and Meryl sat with Aunt Boomerang on a couple of upturned muck buckets in Meryl's grandad's rather crowded allotment shed.

"Old Dipstick still on your backs?" asked Aunt Boomerang.

Sebastian and Meryl nodded.

"He's banned us from going on the school camp," said Meryl glumly, "until we tell him where you're hiding."

"But we're not going to tell him!" declared Sebastian indignantly.

"No way," agreed Meryl.

Aunt Boomerang wiped an imaginary tear from her eye. "Bless you, sweethearts! The important thing now is to get you two off Old Dipstick's blacklist so you can go on the school camp."

"How?" asked Meryl, still glum.

"There must be a way of persuading him of your *good* qualities."

"If there was, he wouldn't take any notice. All he thinks about is the stolen car that's been dumped in the playground," sighed Sebastian. "He's been waiting for ages for the police to tow it away."

"Then that's it!" cried Aunt Boomerang. "You get the car towed away for him! He'll notice that! And it would certainly put you in his good books, wouldn't it?"

"Only one problem," said Meryl glumly. "We haven't got a tow truck."

"True," Aunt Boomerang was forced to admit, "but we know someone who has."

Aunt Boomerang flung open the door and they stepped outside, just in time to see Meryl's grandad arriving in his Chevy pickup truck.

Unfortunately though, they were not in time to see Ashley Belcher racing off down the allotment path, punching the air in front of him in jubilation.

"Enter!" commanded Old Dipstick in response to the sound of the buzzer above his office door.

Ashley Belcher entered.

"Ah, Ashley. I take it, from the triumphant sneer on your face that your mission has been successful."

"Pardon, Sir?"

"The Aunt Boogiebum woman! You've found out where she's hiding?"

"Yes, Sir."

"Then tell me boy ... !"

The next morning dawned brightly. On the allotments, birds sang in the trees. In the large chestnut tree that overlooked Meryl's grandad's shed there sat a family of rooks. In the large chestnut tree that overlooked Meryl's grandad's shed there also sat a mad-eyed figure in a balaclava helmet.

"Get off you!" the mad-eyed figure called to the rooks, whose nest he had violated. "Don't you know who I am? I am Norman Diplock MA, Headmaster, that's who I am!"

The rooks didn't seem impressed by this piece of information. Indeed, one of them squawked, flapped its wings and deposited a large poo right on the end of Old Diplock's nose.

"You're nothing but trouble!" yelled Old Dipstick. "And I don't like trouble! Tomorrow I'm bringing my gun. Do you hear me?" He took a sip from his flask of beef tea. As he trained his binoculars on the allotment shed, Old Dipstick saw Aunt Boomerang coming out. He leaned over to get a better view. Unfortunately, in his excitement, he leaned over too far. Still grasping his flask, he slithered, slipped, then finally fell right off his branch. The family of rooks fell with him. The family of rooks, however, could fly. Old Dipstick couldn't.

"Aargh!" he yelled as he landed with a painful thud on the ground below.

As he struggled to get up, he could feel a damp patch on the seat of his trousers. He looked down and saw he was sitting in a puddle of beef tea.

Half an hour later, Old Dipstick was back in his office. He had twigs in his hair, rook's poo on his nose, beef tea-stained trousers and a bruise on his bottom, but he was smiling. He reckoned such things were a small price to pay for a successful morning's work. Following Ashley's report, he had seen for himself where Aunt Boomerang was hiding out. He had phoned the press, suggesting they should meet him at the allotments straight after school. Not only that, he noted as he strolled to his window, but at last the dumped car was being towed away from his playground.

Sebastian and Meryl called in to see Aunt Boomerang on their way to school. They found her by the large chestnut tree that overlooked the allotment, sniffing.

"Ah ... the spring air," she was enthusing. "I smell blossoms. I smell the dew. I smell compost. I smell beef tea!" She paused. "Beef tea?"

"Grandad doesn't drink beef tea," said Meryl puzzled.

"I'm mighty glad to hear it, sweetheart," replied Aunt Boomerang.

"What kind of person would be so gross as to drink beef tea?" asked Sebastian.

"I don't know, but the grass here is squashed and flat, as if a heavy object has fallen out of the tree onto it," mused Aunt Boomerang, with a slight frown.

Meanwhile, Meryl's grandad was driving his Chevy truck into the school playground. He soon spotted the old and battered car. In no time at all he had hitched it up and was back in his cab.

The sound of the revving engine brought Old Dipstick to his office window.

The sight of the car being towed away brought him racing out of the school.

"Hey, you," he shouted desperately. "Stop! Come back with my car!"

But Meryl's grandad didn't hear him. He was busy singing along to his "Fifty Greatest Party Hits" tape.

His hair still full of twigs and his bottom still damp with beef tea, Old Dipstick set off after the Chevy pickup as fast as his legs would carry him.

Old Dipstick was still pursuing the truck when Meryl's grandad signalled left and turned into the scrapyard. Old Dipstick signalled left too, with his arm, and ran after him.

Meryl's grandad was unhitching Old Dipstick's car when the breathless head teacher finally caught up with him.

"You!" stuttered Old Dipstick, for it was all he could manage to say.

"Me?" asked Meryl's grandad.

"You!" stuttered Meryl's grandad again.

"You've said that once," pointed out Meryl's grandad.

Old Dipstick tried to push Meryl's grandad off his car.

"Hey, what do you think you're doing?" protested Meryl's grandad.

"What do you think *you're* doing?" protested Old Dipstick.

"Bringing this old banger to the dump, where it should have been brought a long time ago by the look of it," replied Meryl's grandad.

"That veteran motor car," fumed Old Dipstick, beside himself with fury, "belongs to *me!*"

Meryl's grandad looked sceptically at Old Dipstick. "What was it doing in the school playground, then?"

Old Dipstick raised himself up to his full height. "Do you know who I am?" he thundered.

Two names suggested themselves to Meryl's grandad. He plumped for the most likely. "Darth Maul?"

"You detestable little man!"

"Quasi Modo, then?"

Old Dipstick growled menacingly. "I am Norman Diplock MA. Headmaster! The car that was dumped in my school playground is being unloaded from the police tow truck over there!"

Meryl's grandad followed Old Dipstick's gaze. "Ah," he said. Then he scratched his chin thoughtfully, but for the life of him could think of nothing else to say.

Sebastian and Meryl were hauled into Old Dipstick's office straight after school.

"I might have guessed it was all your doing. You're trouble! And I don't like trouble! I've thought long and hard about a suitable alternative torture - I mean punishment - for you."

Sebastian and Meryl looked down glumly at the carpet.

"Unfortunately, the thumb screws and rack I ordered from our educational suppliers have yet to arrive." Old Dipstick continued, "So, I thought I'd bar you from school camp. Then I realised I'd already done that!" He giggled hysterically. He seemed to be in his own mad world. "But it doesn't matter, does it? Ha! No! Because I am now in a position to inflict upon you the most spectacular punishment of all! Oh yes, the hour of vengeance is at hand!"

Sebastian was becoming aware of a strange, but curiously familiar, aroma. He sniffed. He glanced across at Meryl and saw that she was sniffing, too.

"What are you snivelling for?" snapped Old Dipstick.

"Beef tea," muttered Meryl in alarm.

"Oh heck," said Sebastian, panic-stricken. He raced from Old Dipstick's office, Meryl close on his heels.

Old Dipstick leant back in his chair. "Aunt Bibbybung, I know where you're hiding. I've got you now!" he roared. He rocked with manic laughter. Indeed, he rocked so much with manic laughter that he tipped over and landed backwards, headfirst in the wastepaper bin.

Sebastian and Meryl raced up through the allotments and landed with a thump, face first, in the rhubarb patch. They looked up to see Meryl's grandad standing above them, chuckling.

"That was blooming great!" he said.

"No it wasn't," argued Meryl.

"I was wondering how I was going to test my New Improved Intruder Trap," Meryl's grandad continued, "when you two came charging along just at the right moment!"

Sebastian and Meryl sat up and saw that they had tripped over a length of string which had been tied between two trees right across the path at ankle height.

Aunt Boomerang came out of the shed.

"G'day, sweethearts!" She frowned at Sebastian and Meryl. "Now, it's not a good idea to lie on the damp ground," she said firmly. "You'll catch your deaths.'

"Aunt Boomerang," said Sebastian in a desperate voice, "Old Dipstick drinks beef tea. That's what we smelt over by the trees. He must have been spying on you!"

"I know," smiled Aunt Boomerang.

"But he'll come up here again, probably with those reporters!" cried Meryl.

"I know that, too. That's why Wally built me that." She indicated a scarecrow, dressed up in some of her clothes.

"A scarecrow?" Sebastian muttered doubtfully. "You think a scarecrow will scare off Old Dipstick?"

"There's my New Improved Intruder Trap as well," Meryl's grandad pointed out.

Suddenly, there was a screech of tyres as a car shot into the allotment road at speed, rocking violently from side to side.

"It must be those car thieves!" yelled Sebastian above the engine roar. "The ones who dumped that car at school! They must've come up here to do their joy riding!"

"Well, what do you know, sweethearts?" declared Aunt

Boomerang. "Who's up for catching a ruthless gang of joy riders red-handed?"

Sebastian and Meryl looked doubtfully at each other.

"How?" asked Sebastian.

"I'd suggest Plan B," said Aunt Boomerang.

"Of course," sighed Sebastian.

"What is Plan B?" asked Meryl.

Aunt Boomerang shrugged. "I don't know."

"Plan B?" said Meryl's grandad gleefully. "Plan B is Wally Daly's Scheme for Catching Joy Riders on an Allotment. All you need is a New Improved Intruder Trap, a cucumber and a bucket of ripe tomatoes. Come on!" And he beckoned the others into the shed to collect their weapons.

Aunt Boomerang, Sebastian, Meryl and Meryl's grandad stormed out of the shed like a commando unit. Each time the stolen car sped past, they pelted the windscreen with ripe tomatoes. The driver screeched to a halt. He and the other joy riders tumbled out and rushed, shouting and cursing, towards Aunt Boomerang.

"Hey, you silly old bat, what do you think you're doing?" yelled the leader, going right up to her.

Aunt Boomerang took a step forward and walked through him. Then she drifted into the surrounding woods and disappeared.

The astounded joy riders stared at her – or rather, they stared at where she had been. Unseen by them, Sebastian,

Meryl and Meryl's grandad stuffed a prize cucumber up the car's exhaust pipe.

"I don't like it," said the biggest of the joy riders. "It's creepy."

"You scared?" the leader asked him.

"Yes!" came the answer.

The joy riders raced back to the car. The driver tried to start the engine. There was a chug-chugging sound and then an almighty bang as the exhaust blew the cucumber out.

The terrified joyriders tumbled out of the car again and decided to run for it. They saw Meryl's grandad, Sebastian and Meryl heading down the road towards them. So they headed up the allotment path.

"Aargh!" they yelled as they each crashed into Meryl's grandad's New Improved Intruder Trap. They toppled to the ground like a row of skittles.

By the time they struggled to their knees, they saw even more people on the scene. Old Dipstick, his hair wild, his eyes mad, was leading a pack of reporters and photographers apparently straight towards them.

"It's a fair cop! I give myself up!" blubbered the biggest of the joy riders. And they got to their knees and put their hands up.

But Old Dipstick raced past them. He wasn't interested in catching a group of joyriders red-handed. He was interested in catching Aunt Boomerang.

"There she is!" he yelled. "I'd recognise that dress any-where!" At full stretch, he threw himself at his quarry. Only when he was on the ground, did he realise that he had just rugby-tackled a scarecrow.

"She's up here somewhere! I saw her with by own eyes! She's trouble! And I don't like trouble."

He looked round and saw that he was talking to himself. The reporters and photographers were busily talking to Meryl's grandad, Sebastian and Meryl, taking pictures of them as the police led the joy riders away.

The full page photospread in the paper next day was cap-tioned "Young Have-a-Go Heroes Catch Joy Riders!".

Aunt Boomerang looked fondly at the photo. "Ah, don't I look lovely, sweethearts?" she gushed. For standing behind the two "Have-a-Go Heroes" was standing the beaming ghost of an Australian soap star.

"The police sergeant said he'll have a word with Old Dipstick and tell him we should be allowed to go on the school camp, seeing as we're local heroes," said Sebastian.

"Bonza!" said Aunt Boomerang.

Outside, Meryl's grandad was shovelling steaming horse manure from one pile to another.

"I don't know," said Meryl's grandad, "I can't see how this stuff is going to rot down any more quickly over here than it was over there. I think I've been wasting my time!"

"On the contrary," said Aunt Boomerang. "Look how your new heap under the hedge is hotting up. Why, it's visibly moving with the heat!"

Meryl's grandad, Sebastian and Meryl looked. "Moving?" frowned Sebastian. "That manure heap isn't moving, it's *heaving!*"

"Aargh!" cried Meryl suddenly. "There must be a creature in there! A rat or something!" And she raced back to the safety of the shed.

"Blooming 'eck!" declared Meryl's grandad. "Whatever it is, it's bigger than a rat. Look at the way that heap is swelling. I'm off!" And Meryl's grandad raced back to the safety of the shed, closely followed by Sebastian.

Aunt Boomerang chuckled to herself, then drifted through the shed door to join the others.

"If you can bring yourselves to do it, just take a look through the window, sweethearts," she suggested.

Gingerly, Meryl's grandad, Sebastian and Meryl raised their eyes to the level of the window.

"Well, I'll be jiggered," gasped Meryl's grandad.

"Wow!" gasped Meryl.

"Cor!" gasped Sebastian.

Staggering from the rotting, steaming, smelly manure heap was a familiar figure. A familiar figure whose wild eyes stared out from the opening of a balaclava helmet. A familiar figure who shook his fist at the allotment shed, as great dollops of horse dung fell from his arm.

"I know you're in there, barmy Aunt Bangeroom!" growled Old Dipstick. "And I'm going to get you! Oh yes, I'm going to get you!"

Chapter 6

A FÊTE WORSE THAN DEATH

6

A Fête Worse Than Death

"I'm going to get you! Oh yes, I'm going to get you!"

Old Dipstick stood in his office, holding a brand new shining dart in his hand. He screwed up his eyes fiercely at the target on the opposite wall. In the centre of this target was a newspaper photo. The headline above the photo was "Young Have-a-Go Heroes Catch Joy Riders!".

Old Dipstick's eyes focused on the bit of the photo that showed Aunt Boomerang's smiling face.

"Concentrate, Norman," snapped Mrs Belcher, who was sitting in the head teacher's chair. "Think of all that she has done to humiliate you. Think of your shrunken referee's kit ... the shower in the wardrobe ... the flour ball ... the manure heap!"

Old Dipstick grunted.

"Take aim!"

Old Dipstick took aim. The dart sailed in a fast, straight line to the opposite wall. It struck the photo, right on the end of Aunt Boomerang's nose. And stayed there.

"Ha!" cried Old Dipstick triumphantly. "I'm going to get you!"

"The bell will soon be going for end of school," Mrs Belcher said. "Time for your evening watch at the allotments." She opened the cupboard door, took out a camouflage suit and handed it to Old Dipstick.

Ms Goodbody was handing out leaflets about the school fête.

"It's this Saturday. We need lots of money for the School Fund. I'm doing my bit for the cause, even though my boyfriend Erik is over from Sweden for the weekend."

At the sound of Erik's name, the class erupted into whoops and cheers. Ms Goodbody blushed.

"Is he good looking, Miss?" asked Jodie.

"Of course he is!" answered Ms Goodbody indignantly.

"Can we meet him, Miss?" asked Meryl.

"Yes!" Ms Goodbody paused and grinned. "If you come and help at the fête that is."

"Wow," said Meryl.

"What does he do?" asked Jodie.

"He buys Scottish craft and takes it back to Sweden to sell," replied Ms Goodbody. "In fact, I'm travelling back to Sweden with him for half term," she added, with a faraway look in her eyes.

"Wow," said Meryl.

Ms Goodbody was suddenly catapulted out of her daydream by the shrill, incessant ringing of the school bell. The class began to shuffle in their seats.

"I hope all of you get involved with the fête and raise lots of money for the School Fund! And I want all your parents – and Aunts – " Ms Goodbody cast a meaningful look at Sebastian, " – helping too."

The Simpkins' kitchen was crammed with pots. Big pots, small pots, flower pots, tea pots. Mr Simpkins was getting into pottery in a serious way. Sebastian handed him the leaflet about the school fête.

"I'd be happy to help," he said. "I'll make some special pottery."

Sebastian frowned uneasily. "Er … it doesn't have to be anything special, Dad. A couple of mugs would do."

But there was a determined glint in Mr Simpkins' eye. "Oh … it'll be special all right. This is my big chance to show that miserable head teacher of yours that when it comes to fund raising, Kevin Simpkins can pull his weight!"

"Oh dear," sighed Sebastian.

He found his mum in Aunt Boomerang's old room, wiring something electrical to the sash window.

"It's a Remote Control Window Shutting Device," explained Mrs Simpkins. She pressed a zapper and the window suddenly shut fast with a sickening thud. Sebastian jumped.

" … It's for Aunt Boomerang, if she ever comes to stay again. It would be wonderful if she did, wouldn't it?" Mrs

Simpkins said wistfully. She looked up from reading the fête leaflet. "Fund raising, eh? Now what shall I make?"

"Er ... no need to put yourself out, Mum, if you're busy," he said desperately. "A nice pair of wooden bookends would do."

"Bookends?" retorted Mrs Simpkins. "This is my big chance to show the snooty Chair of the School Governors Scraggie Maggie Belcher, just what I'm capable of!"

"Oh dear," sighed Sebastian.

"They're bound to make something really embarrassing, both of them," explained Sebastian. He and Meryl were sitting in the allotment shed with Meryl's grandad, Aunt Boomerang and Prince Charles - Meryl's grandad's whippet.

"School fête, eh?" declared Aunt Boomerang. "Bonza idea!"

"The School Fund's short of money," said Meryl glumly.

"I'm not surprised," exclaimed Aunt Boomerang. "Where do you think the cash for all those plants in Old Dipstick's office came from?"

"Why, the tight-fisted old crook!" roared Meryl's grandad. "Well, I've got plenty of rhubarb you can sell."

"Thanks, grandad," said Meryl uncertainly.

"I'd love to run a stall or something," murmured Aunt Boomerang.

"But, Aunt Boomerang, you're in hiding!" Sebastian

protested. "Suppose someone saw you?"

"If I was in disguise ... and in a darkened tent with a veil covering my face, they'd have no chance of seeing me," smiled Aunt Boomerang. "I shall be 'Madame Zsa Zsa Bestingo' - Fortune Teller! I can read tea leaves, you know. It's an old skill I learnt from the native Australians."

"Wow!" said Meryl. She handed Aunt Boomerang one of her grandad's mugs. "What do the tea leaves in the bottom of that mug tell you?"

Aunt Boomerang peered at the mouldy pile of pap in the bottom of the mug and curled up her nose. "What these tea leaves tell me is that your grandad hasn't done his washing up for a month!"

Meryl's grandad looked a bit sheepish. "Aw, I never bother about a bit of mould myself," he shrugged. "Mould contains penicillin. And penicillin's good for you."

Aunt Boomerang shot him a frosty look. Meryl's grandad took the mug and emptied the mucky tea leaves into an even muckier bowl of slops. He opened the shed window and flung the lot out.

"Awror!" came a muffled cry from directly underneath the window. Old Dipstick, who was hiding there, picked mouldy tea leaves and rotting potato peelings from his hair.

"Fortune teller at the school fête! Ha! I've got her now - and on my home ground! Oh yes! Barmy Aunt Bingybomby, I've got you now!"

It was the day of school fête. Mr Simpkins stood by his stall, busily dusting the two hundred and fifty six pots he had managed to make. Old Dipstick stood nearby, smirking at the blue and white striped tent that was to be home to "Madame Zsa Zsa Bestingo" for the next two hours.

Over in the woods which bordered one side of the field, Mrs Simpkins was putting the finishing touches to an aerial ropeway. It stretched across a deep-sided pit which had been dug many years ago when the soil had been needed to level the playing fields.

Mrs Simpkins tightened the last bolt and went across to the field to join the crowd which had gathered to watch Councillor Mrs Margaret Belcher perform the opening ceremony. A familiar head popped up from the bushes and grinned the kind of evil little grin you can only manage if you're a genuine numero uno ugly brute and bully.

"I'll teach that Sebastian Simpkins to mess with me," muttered Ashley Belcher darkly. He took a spanner from his pocket and undid one of the retaining bolts on Mrs Simpkins' aerial ropeway.

Meryl found Ms Goodbody and her boyfriend looking at Mr Simpkins' pots.

"Meryl," called Ms Goodbody. "This is Erik."

"Wow!" said Meryl. She stared up at a handsome, bronzed

face and found her gaze met by the pair of bluest eyes she had ever seen.

"Erik's going to buy some of Sebastian's father's pots. He's taking them back to Sweden to sell in his craft shop!"

"Wow!" said Meryl.

Sebastian nudged her. "Come on, Merry. Let's go and have our fortunes told by Madame Zsa Zsa Bestingo."

Meryl sighed. "I think the future's best left untold," she said gloomily.

"Rubbish," declared Sebastian. "I thought today would be terrible, what with Dad's pots and Mum's DIY. But Dad's made a great deal with Erik and Mum's aerial ropeway looks fantastic. I think today's one of those days when everything is going to go right."

Which goes to show just how wrong you can be. Even after you've been turned into a daredevil by the ghost of an Australian soap star.

Standing by Mr Simpkins' pottery stall, Mrs Belcher and Old Dipstick watched Aunt Boomerang's blue and white striped tent.

"I've got her, Margaret! I've got her this time!"

"Are you sure you don't need a hand, Norman?" enquired Mrs Belcher.

"That is most kind of you, Margaret, but no. Thank you." From his pocket, Old Dipstick took out a pair of handcuffs

and a rope. "There are some things a man has to do ... alone!"
And he moved off towards Aunt Boomerang's tent.

Mrs Belcher turned to find Ashley by her side.

"Oh, Ashley, my little lamb, are you helping by writing
signs for the sideshows?"

Ashley held a stick of chalk in one hand. It was worn at
one end, from where he had just rubbed out the word
"BUY" from Mr Simpkins' "BUY A POT" sign and replaced
it with the word "'SMASH".

"Er ... no, mum – "

"Oh, don't be so modest, Ashley! 'SMASH A POT', eh?"
she read.

"No, Mum!"

"But Ashley, I am Chair of the School Governors. It's my
duty to have a go at every sideshow!" She picked up a hard
wooden ball from the neighbouring coconut shy and hurled
it at one of Mr Simpkins' biggest pots.

There was a dull thud as the ball hit the pot, then a crash
as the pot smashed into tiny pieces.

"Ye-es!" boomed Mrs Belcher. "Do I win a prize?" she
asked an astonished Mr Simpkins.

"That pot ..." he stammered, " ... that pot was worth fifty
pounds!"

"Aw, stop whingeing man, it's a 'Smash the Pot' stall, isn't
it?"

Mr Simpkins saw the sign. Then he saw Ashley, who was

busily trying to stuff the stick of chalk up his tee-shirt.

"Hey, you!" he shouted at Ashley.

"Ashley!" shouted Mrs Belcher.

But Ashley had gone. Racing away as fast as he could, towards the blue and white striped tent in the middle of the field.

Aunt Boomerang frowned at a saucer of tea leaves.

"Hmm," she said to Meryl. "I see ominous portents."

"Oh dear," said Meryl.

"I see clouds gathering on the horizon."

"Oh dear," said Meryl.

"I see ... "

Aunt Boomerang looked up from the saucer and saw a grinning face by the tent door. The kind of evil grinning face you can only manage if you're a genuine numero uno ugly brute and bully.

"I see ... Ashley Belcher!"

Out of the tent flew Ashley, straight back to Mr Simpkins' stall, where his mum was unhappily depositing a fifty pound note in Mr Simpkins' outstretched hand.

"Mum," stammered Ashley breathlessly, "I've got something to tell you!"

Mrs Belcher glowered at her son, put her pimply face next to his and hissed, "Out of my sight, you idiot boy!"

Round the back of the blue and white striped tent stood

Meryl and Sebastian.

"Coast is clear!" whispered Sebastian.

Through the tent wall Aunt Boomerang appeared.

"Come on!" called Meryl. "We've got to get you away, before Ashley finds you!"

By the front door of the tent stood Old Dipstick, handcuffs in one hand, rope in the other. Into the darkened tent he went.

At the side of the tent stood Ashley. He pulled one guy line from its peg, then another, and another and another. The tent crashed to the ground.

"Awror!" called a muffled and startled voice from inside.

Mrs Belcher was already running to the scene.

"Mum!" yelled a triumphant Ashley. "We've caught Simpkins' barmy Aunt Boomerang! She was Madame Zsa Zsa Bestingo! See ... ?"

But from out from under the tent crawled, not the ghost of an Australian soap star, but a head teacher.

"Ashley...?" said Mrs Belcher in a trembling voice.

"Ashley!" shrieked Old Dipstick in a not-so-trembling voice.

And they both made a grab for the wretched numero uno ugly brute and bully.

"There they go!" screamed Ashley, stepping quickly to

one side. And, indeed, heading across the school field towards the woods could be seen Meryl, closely followed by Sebastian and Aunt Boomerang.

Through Mr Simpkins' pottery stall raced Ashley, Mrs Belcher and Old Dipstick, sending Mr Simpkins diving in all directions to save his tumbling pots from smashing on the ground.

Through the refreshment stall raced Ashley, Mrs Belcher and Old Dipstick, soaking everyone in tea, orange squash and elderflower wine.

Through the second hand clothes stall raced Ashley, Mrs Belcher and Old Dipstick, getting themselves covered in woolly scarves and fancy silk blouses.

By the time they reached the woods, they were gaining on Aunt Boomerang, Meryl and Sebastian.

Mrs Simpkins was standing by her aerial ropeway. "Aunt Boomerang! Grab this!" she yelled frantically. She threw Aunt Boomerang the rope.

Aunt Boomerang grabbed it. She sailed away over the deep pit the rope was strung across. As soon as she reached the other side, the rope ran back across the pit on its well-oiled pulley.

Old Dipstick grabbed it and immediately began to glide across the pit. Suddenly there was the sound of a long, loud crack. The rope gave way and the ropeway and Old Dipstick toppled helplessly into the pit below.

"Awror!" cried Old Dipstick, for the second time that day.

"This is your doing Tracey Simpkins!" thundered Mrs Belcher.

"Oh no it's not! Look, the bolt's been undone," Mrs Simpkins pointed out.

"Ashley!" Old Dipstick crawled like a swamp monster up the sides of the pit and grabbed the numero uno ugly brute and bully by the collar. "Find the Bongerboom woman. Or I'll personally tie you up by your ears to this ropeway!"

"Did you hear what I said, Ashley?" cried Old Dipstick.

Ashley heard.

Sebastian and Meryl collapsed on the allotment shed floor and tried to get their breath back. Aunt Boomerang lay on the bed, completely still.

"Sweethearts!" she said weakly. "I'm getting too old for all this sort of thing."

"Too old?" exclaimed Sebastian incredulously. "Aunt Boomerang, you're a ghost. Ghosts don't get old!"

"Sometimes even a ghost needs to rest in peace. Go out and guard the door will you?" Aunt Boomerang shivered, as if she was feeling the cold. "They know I'm up here."

Even as Aunt Boomerang spoke, there was a sound of scuffling outside the shed door.

Sebeastian felt Meryl grasp his hand. "I forgot to lock the door!" she whispered in alarm.

Sebastian saw that, indeed, the door was ajar. Slowly, it began to inch open. Aunt Boomerang lay on the bed shivering.

Then in through the door came ...

"Prince Charles!" exclaimed Meryl.

Prince Charles wagged his tail, then nuzzled Meryl's hand.

"You'll be safe enough now, Aunt Boomerang," said Sebastian. "You've got a guard dog to protect you."

"Guard dog?" smiled Aunt Boomerang weakly. "*Lard* dog, more like. He won't even move himself to chase a rabbit off the allotment. Just sits there like a tub of lard."

"Aunt Boomerang's right," sighed Meryl. "Prince Charles is a retired dog. He's had it with barking and growling and chasing off intruders."

As if to prove Meryl's point, Prince Charles stretched his legs, then curled up at the foot of the bed with his paws over his ears.

"But Aunt Boomerang!" pleaded Sebastian. "You can't let Ashley and Old Dipstick find you! You've got to disappear!"

"Not in the state I'm in, sweetheart. I just haven't got the *energy* to disappear. Now, just let me rest and whatever you do, don't let anyone in."

Sebastian and Meryl opened the door and peered out. There was no sign of Old Dipstick, Mrs Belcher or Ashley.

"And take that ugly, great thing with you!"

She pointed to the corner of the shed where one of Mr Simpkins' larger pots stood.

"Your grandad bought it for me, as a token of his esteem," Aunt Boomerang whispered to Meryl.

"He never did!" exclaimed Meryl incredulously.

"No ..." Aunt Boomerang managed a small chuckle. "He bought it to keep his spuds in."

Sebastian and Meryl sat on Mr Simpkins' pot, guarding the shed. The sun had disappeared behind some low cloud and a chilly wind had started to blow. There was nobody else on the allotments. It was completely quiet, but both Sebastian and Meryl knew that it wouldn't stay that way for long.

"She knows, doesn't she?" Meryl said quietly. "She saw it in those tea leaves. Something mega awful's going to happen." She tensed. "It's High Noon, Sebby."

"It's the highest of High Noons," whispered Sebastian urgently. "And Aunt Boomerang can't help us this time."

Meryl followed Sebastian's gaze across the allotments to the gate. Ashley Belcher was approaching. He looked determined and threatening.

"Get back in the shed with Aunt Boomerang - just in case I can't keep him out," Sebastian told Meryl. He walked down the allotment towards Ashley. The two boys stood facing each other. Sebastian could see Ashley's smirk and his sneering eyes.

"So, it's just you and me is it, Simpkins?"

Sebastian nodded.

"You'd save yourself a lot of bother if just let me in the shed. I know she's in there."

Sebastian looked Ashley in the eye and held his look.

"You won't get past me, Ashley."

"I will," answered Ashley. "You're a scaredy-cat."

"Not any more, I'm not. And you know it."

Something about Sebastian's apparently calm manner was unnerving Ashley. "I'm going in that shed. I'm going to keep that barmy old bat in there until my mum and Mr Diplock get here," he declared, but there was a strange hesitation in his voice.

Sebastian continued to hold Ashley's look. Ashley looked away.

"But I've got to get her!" cried Ashley, desperately. "Or else Mr Diplock is going to string me up by the ears from your mum's aerial ropeway!"

"Just go," said Sebastian quietly.

Suddenly, Ashley made a rush for the shed. Wrong-footed, Sebastian was slow off the mark to grab him. Ashley had just got his hand on the shed door handle, when something slithered off the roof and straight onto his head. It was Mr Simpkins' pot.

"Awror!" came Ashley's muffled voice from inside the pot.

"Merry?" gasped a startled Sebastian as he saw his friend's frowning face peering over the roof edge.

"Did I get him?" she asked.

"Awror!" said Ashley, his head stuck fast inside the pot.

The shed door crashed open, "Sweethearts," ordered a cross voice, "keep the noise down, would you? I'm trying to rest!" Only then did Aunt Boomerang see Ashley's feet sticking out the bottom of the pot. "Strewth!" she said.

There was a screech of brakes as Meryl's grandad's Chevy pulled up. He leapt out and raced up to them.

"I saw the chase up on the school field," he said. "Looked as if there might be trouble, so I raced up here."

"You're too late," sighed Meryl.

"That's a mighty funny-looking potato," frowned Meryl's grandad, studying Ashley's feet.

"Awror!" said Ashley.

"Come on, Aunt Boomerang, time to go," said Sebastian.

"Go where?" asked Aunt Boomerang.

"Home," said Sebastian quietly, but firmly. "Mum and Dad miss you." He paused. "And so do I."

They loaded Aunt Boomerang's cases into Meryl's grandad's Chevy. Prince Charles ambled out of the shed and hauled himself up into the cab.

"Looks like we were just in time," said Meryl's grandad as Old Dipstick's car roared up behind them.

"Awror!" said Ashley, from inside the pot.

Sitting next to Old Dipstick in his car, Mrs Belcher looked out of the window and straightaway saw Ashley with a pot on his shoulders where his head should have been. She leapt out of the car.

"Oh my goodness, what have they done to my little lamb?" she said to Ashley - or rather to the pot he was in.

"Awror!" replied Ashley.

Mrs Belcher struggled to pull the pot off Ashley's head. "Norman! Give me a hand!" she called. She looked up to see Old Dipstick driving off after Meryl's grandad's Chevy.

"Stuff Ashley!" yelled Old Dipstick.

Aunt Boomerang, Meryl's grandad, Ms Goodbody, Erik, Meryl, Sebastian, Mr Simpkins and Mrs Simpkins all gathered in the kitchen amongst Mr Simpkins' pots and Aunt Boomerang's suitcases.

"Kev, Trace," said Aunt Boomerang, eyeing the hundreds of pots, "you sure you've got room for me?"

"The pots are all going," explained Mr Simpkins. "Erik says they'll fetch hundreds in Sweden."

"Strewth!" muttered Aunt Boomerang.

Erik and Mr Simpkins began to move the pots out on a trolley.

"Your room's all ready, Aunt Boomerang," said Mrs Simpkins. "I've even installed a special Remote Control

Window Shutting Device for you!"

"Bonza, sweetheart," smiled Aunt Boomerang.

Aunt Boomerang lay on her bed. She was busy pressing the buttons on her Remote Control Window Shutting Device zapper, so she didn't see Old Dipstick leering in at the window. She pushed the big red button. Suddenly, the window slammed down shut with a sickening thud.

"Aargh!" yelled Old Dipstick as he pulled his hands away, just in time.

However, in pulling his hands away so quickly, he lost his footing on the ladder he had climbed to get into Aunt Boomerang's room.

He slithered down to the ground.

Unfortunately, this was precisely where Mr Simpkins and Erik had left the trolley they had been using for loading Erik's van. Old Dipstick landed, tummy-first on the trolley.

The trolley began to roll down the path. It gathered speed. It rolled straight onto the drive, across the pavement and into the back of Erik's van.

There was a resounding thud, a muffled cry and then silence.

Erik and Ms Goodbody came out of the front door. They shut the tailgate of the van and got into the cab.

"Awror!" groaned Old Dipstick, but they didn't hear him because Erik had just started the engine.

"Next stop, Stockholm," smiled Ms Goodbody.

"Goodbye, sweethearts!" called Aunt Boomerang. She, Mr and Mrs Simpkins, Sebastian and Meryl stood at the gate and waved until Erik's van disappeared from sight.

Aunt Boomerang turned and breathed in the warm evening air. She looked up at the odd little semi-detached house with its pointy gables and wonky chimney. Yes, she *had* grown fond of it. No, more than that, she felt as if she *belonged* here.

"Sweethearts," she said, smiling broadly at Mr and Mrs Simpkins, Sebastian and Meryl, "it is really bonza to be home!"

As Erik and Ms Goodbody drove through that part of the city where the roads are wider and the cars are smarter, a voice in the back of the van chortled crazily, "I'm going to get you Aunt Boomerang! You're trouble! And I don't like trouble!"

But Old Dipstick's only audience was two hundred and fifty four home-made pots.

Based on the BBC TV series
"Barmy Aunt Boomerang" by Roy Apps

Aunt Boomerang	Toyah Willcox
Sebastian Simpkins	Richard Madden
Tracey Simpkins, his mother	Sharon Mackenzie
Kevin Simpkins, his father	Lawrie McNicol
Meryl McIntosh, his pal	Laura McKenzie
Renne McIntosh, her mother	Annette Staines
Wally Daly, her grandfather	James Martin
Norman Diplock, headteacher	Kern Falconer
Ashley Belcher, the bully	Blain Slater
Nozza McRory, his pal	Darren Brownlee
Rozza McRory, his twin	David Brownlee
Margaret Belcher, Ashley's mother	Terry Neason
Sabrina Goodbody, teacher – class P7	Susy Kane
School Inspector	Alasdair Cording
Jodie, Meryl's pal	Harriet Lunney
Pandora, Meryl's pal	Emma Murphy
Wee Hamish	Ian De Caestecker
Sarah	Jennifer Fergie
Jasminder	Omar Yamin

Executive Producer	Claire Mundell
Producer	John Adams
Directors	Brian Kelly
	Michael Hines
Editor	Peter Hayes

A BBC Scotland production for CBBC

ROY APPS

Roy Apps was born in Kent. He trained and worked as a teacher, but was released thirteen years ago. Since then, he has written thirty four books for children, sixty odd television scripts and sixty not-so-odd ones. He is perhaps best known for his How To Handle books. He launched the latest title in the series, How to Handle Your Teacher, at the Edinburgh Book Festival this year. His novel about British film pioneers, The Secret Summer of Daniel Lyons won the Writers Guild Award for Best Children's Book of 1992 and was runner up in the Whitbread Awards in the same year. Frankie Stein's Robot has been shortlisted for the 1999 Nottinghamshire Children's Book Award.

For the last seven years, he has been a scriptwriter on the BBC children's dramer Byker Grove and, of course, he created and wrote Barmy Aunt Boomerang for BBC Scotland. He lives in Brighton with his wife and two young sons.

READ MORE LIMERICK BOOKS, CD'S AND TAPES

NEW IMPROVED LIMERICKS

POEMS TO SHOUT OUT LOUD

NOT MORE POEMS TO SHOUT OUT LOUD

THE NEW ADVENTURES OF PHIL & LILL

MORE ADVENTURES OF PHIL & LILL

MISERABLE POEMS

AUDIO CASSETTES

POEMS TO SHOUT OUT LOUD (EMI RECORDS)

RUB-A-DUB-DUB (EMI RECORDS)

NEW IMPROVED LIMERICKS LIVE!